Note for Librarians: A cataloguing record for this book is available from Library and Archives Canada at www.collectionscanada.ca/amicus/index-e.html
ISBN 1-4120-7653-6

Printed in Victoria, BC, Canada. Printed on paper with minimum 30% recycled fibre. Trafford's print shop runs on "green energy" from solar, wind and other environmentally-friendly power sources.

PUBLISHING™
Offices in Canada, USA, Ireland and UK
This book was published *on-demand* in cooperation with Trafford Publishing. On-demand publishing is a unique process and service of making a book available for retail sale to the public taking advantage of on-demand manufacturing and Internet marketing. On-demand publishing includes promotions, retail sales, manufacturing, order fulfilment, accounting and collecting royalties on behalf of the author.

Book sales for North America and international:
Trafford Publishing, 6E–2333 Government St.,
Victoria, BC v8t 4p4 CANADA
phone 250 383 6864 (toll-free 1 888 232 4444)
fax 250 383 6804; email to orders@trafford.com
Book sales in Europe:
Trafford Publishing (uk) Limited, 9 Park End Street, 2nd Floor
Oxford, UK oxi ihh UNITED KINGDOM
phone 44 (0)1865 722 113 (local rate 0845 230 9601)
facsimile 44 (0)1865 722 868; info.uk@trafford.com
Order online at:
trafford.com/05-2548

10 9 8 7 6 5 4 3 2 1

Once Upon
A Horse

For Lainy ~
    From one kind of artist
to another!
            Sheila Watson
                Jan. 06

This book is dedicated to my riding buddies,
with thanks for the many campfires, trails,
and adventures shared.

CHAPTER ONE

"Come here, you damn cat!" I spat out in exasperation, and then in a more cajoling tone pleaded, "Here kitty, kitty, kitty." I felt as limp as a wet noodle in a hot pot on that sweltering August afternoon. Crawling under and through the tangled mass of lilac bushes that bordered our newly purchased acreage near Abbotsford, B.C. in pursuit of the cat wasn't exactly what I had planned for today.

Ying Yang, my Siamese cat, was having too much fun being a country feline instead of being cooped up in a house on a narrow lot in the West End of Vancouver. She was after the sparrows that kept up a lively chit- chat in the undergrowth of the bushes. With her dark chocolate color blending into the shadows and her sneaky approach, she had managed to seize one of the unsuspecting little birds. Now, I was trying to catch her to release the tiny creature before she damaged it.

"Come on, Ying-Yang," I coaxed, "Give it to me...there's a good kitty." I crawled a few more feet, then dropped to my belly and slid along in the dust, reaching out for the mighty hunter who remained just beyond my grasp. Twigs snagged my long, dark- blond hair, sweat ran down between my squashed breasts,

1

and my knee scraped over a sharp rock as I made a lunge and grabbed the cat by the scruff of her neck.
Gotcha, you bugger!" I shouted, as I backed out of the bushes onto the driveway, clutching the cat to my chest. I quickly inserted a finger into the side of her mouth, pried open her jaw, and dropped the stunned little bird into my hand.

A loud snort and a whoosh of air blasted the hair on my neck, making me whirl in alarm and land on my butt. I was facing a pair of trim, black legs with the feet neatly shod. A horse and rider stood in my driveway, and had obviously been watching my antics. The beautiful buckskin lowered his head and snorted again. Clumsily, I stood up, brushing the dust from my jeans, and looked up into the grinning face of the gelding's rider. He was about my age and very good looking. He sat his horse with nonchalant ease, and was having a tough time trying not to burst out laughing. *"Oh damn! Why did I have to look like this?* I thought as I blushed scarlet and fumbled for words.

"Uh....hi...I'm Lindsey Wakefield......and this is Ying Yang... I had to rescue the sparrow," I finished lamely as I put the cat on the ground and shooed her off. I held out my hand so

2

the rider could see the sparrow. "I think it's gonna be okay."

"Yeah," the rider spoke. "That was quite a rescue operation." His blue eyes fairly glittered with amusement. He wore an Australian type cowboy hat with a leather string held by a bead under his square chin. His denim shirt was open at the throat, showing brown skin to match his tanned face. Dark, curly hair spilled out from under his hat, and he had sideburns.

Wow! Sideburns. I thought. *I haven't seen those since Elvis was all the rage. Who is this guy?*

As if reading my thoughts, he leaned forward in the saddle and said, "I'm Russell Livingston...we have the dairy farm at the end of the road. You can see the silos from here."

Although I had seen them and knew where the farm was, I looked up the road anyway. "It's nice to meet you," I stammered. I was still cringing with embarrassment at my appearance. My face was hot, bits of leaves and twigs were imbedded at crazy angles in my hair, dirt streaked my jeans, and to my horror, I suddenly noticed that the buttons on my blue cotton shirt were done up wrong.

Russell either didn't notice my discomfort, or didn't really care that I was a mess, as he continued to sit on his horse, looking down at me. The corners of his mouth still twitched in a grin, but he had control of himself now. "My mom said she saw you schooling a horse in your riding ring a couple of days ago, and I got curious to see who you were, so I took a ride over. Hope you don't mind me being nosy."

"Not at all," I gushed. "My mom and I just moved in here last weekend, and I didn't really expect to meet anyone until I started school."

The tiny bird in my hand fluffed up its feathers and chirruped. I held my hand out flat as it somewhat unsteadily wobbled out onto my fingers. It flapped its tiny wings once, and then took off into the safety of the lilac bushes. "Mission accomplished." I grinned. Ying Yang was off on other adventures.

"What grade are you in?" asked Russell.

"I'm in twelve, my last year," I replied.

"Hey, no way. Me too." Russell straightened up in the saddle. "We'll be on the bus together. You're going to Abbey High, right?"

I nodded in the affirmative, and gave him my best smile. "That's great!" And I meant it. I had been feeling pretty insecure about riding the strange school bus and attending a brand new school, after going to Kitsilano High in Vancouver for the past five years.

With the bird gone, my hands were now free. I reached out and ran my fingers along the muscular neck of Russell's horse. The gelding turned his head and sniffed my shirt. "Your horse is beautiful," I said, stroking the golden coat. "What's his name?"

With obvious pride, the young cowboy replied, "Oh, he's got a fancy name in the Quarter Horse Association, but I call him Sundance, or just Sunny."

"That's real nice," I said, and then added, "Would you like to come and see my horse?"

"Sure," Russell replied. He swung down off his horse with an easy grace. Looping the reins over his arm, horse and boy fell into step beside me as I turned towards the house.

As we passed through the yard, which was overgrown with neglect, the big yellow Lab that had been sleeping in the sun on the back porch came to life. With hackles up, barking enthusiastically, Buckwheat came on the run to ward off the intruder. It wasn't often he was caught napping, and he was trying his best to remedy the situation. I quickly shushed him, and then just to show off, I said, "Buck, you're fired as watchdog around here." For some reason, that dog loved the ground I walked upon, and always had his eye on me. I pointed my finger at him and said, "Bang!"

Buckwheat dropped to the ground, rolled over and lay still, except for his tail that kept on thumping the ground. As soon as I said, "Okay!" he jumped up and literally bounced up and down in excitement.

Russell was suitably impressed and made a big fuss of the dog. Then he tied Sunny to the back fence with his hackamore rope before we slipped through the wires of the five-acre pasture where my mare grazed. I whistled softly as we approached, and Red lifted her head, pricked her ears and stood alert, watching us. I, in turn, watched Russell for his reaction. If he were as good a judge of horseflesh as I thought he was, he would like Red. I liked what I saw – respect and admiration in his eyes as he stood waiting for her to come to us.

"Wow! Is she a racehorse, or something?" Russell asked. "She's built like a Greyhound."

I laughed. "Actually, she is.... or was. She won her maiden race at Exhibition Park as a two year old, but she bowed a tendon on her right front soon after. A friend of mine at school knew her trainer, and heard that she was going to be sent to the glue factory. Red's owner didn't have the money to board her out for the long recovery process, so he had

to get rid of her. I offered him five
hundred dollars and he was glad to get it.
I had to work hard at the stable in
Richmond to pay for her board, and I
couldn't ride her for a year, but she was
worth the wait. I've been pestering my
mom for the past two years to move out
to the country so that I could have Red
outside my door, instead of having to
take the bus out to the stables to see
her."

 The gorgeous young red chestnut
mare with the small white star came to
investigate her visitors. She was
lonesome in the pasture all by herself and
welcomed company. She had always been
part of a herd – first at Lavender Stock
Farm where she was born, then at the
track, and after her injury, at the
boarding stable.

 "She has a fancy name too," I told
Russell, as I patted Red's shoulder. She's
in the Thoroughbred Registry as Doc's
Dancing Doll, but I christened her
Redwing. Her legs are her wings, and one
was injured so she couldn't fly or run like
the wind. Of course, being such a bright
red chestnut, the name just seemed to
fit."

 "It's pretty, and so is she," Russell
said. He looked at me sideways, and I got
the feeling that he thought I was kind of
pretty too. My blue eyes were a match for
his in depth and color, and I was slim. In

fact, I used to be called 'beanpole' in Jr.
High. Stupidly, I blushed again. I started
talking to cover my shyness. "I'm hoping
to show her in Hunter/Jumper classes
next year, and I would love to do Three
Day Eventing. Only... I'm not sure if her
tendon will hold up. I'd like to raise some
foals from her and start a riding school
someday. I really want to work with
horses. I'm just not sure how to go about
it. Mom says I need to get a real job like a
nurse or teacher, or something. What
about you? What do you want to do after
graduation?"

Russell continued to study the
mare. He liked her large, soft eyes, with
the wide space between them showing
her intelligence; he liked the way her
arched neck and deep chest fit into the
sharp withers and the athletic body, her
long legs that were built for running, and
her powerful rear end. She was a beauty.

I waited for an answer. In time, I
would come to realize that Russell's
silences weren't empty. He was thinking.
He didn't just talk for the sake of talking.
I was pretty quiet myself, and I was
secretly delighted to meet such a
handsome, nice young guy who was
going to be our neighbor. This move was
going to be a good one.

Russell squatted, and ran his hands
down the mare's front legs feeling where
the bowed tendon had been. "She's made

a good recovery," he said. "There's not much of a bump left. How long ago was it?"

"She's five now, so it was two and a half years ago," I told him. Redwing snuffed Russell's hat as he examined the foot. Then he stood again and looked into my eyes.

"I thought I might like to be a horse doctor...you know, a vet. But it's such a long grind at Vet School, and you have to work a long time to pay off your debts. I work for my dad milking cows and doing fieldwork. My brother Danny isn't interested in the farm, so I guess I could take it over some day. People will always need dairy products and it's a good living." He sighed. "I haven't really decided yet."

"Yeah, me neither," I said. "I guess there's lots of time for that."

We turned and walked back to where Russell had left Sunny. Redwing followed us and I was surprised that she hadn't noticed that there was a strange horse in the yard. No sooner had that thought entered my head, than Redwing suddenly threw up her head and whinnied loudly. She charged past Russell and I and galloped up to the fence, flinging clods of grass and dirt up under her churning hooves. She had spied Sundance.

Sunny was out of reach, but was excited too. He lifted his head and whinnied back at this new friend. He rolled his eyes and snorted through his nose, while pawing the ground in excitement.

Russell laughed. "Looks like our horses want to get together too. Do you trail ride her, or is she just an arena horse?"

"Oh", I answered, "I love to trail ride, and she's actually getting pretty good. She was an awful klutz at first with deadfall and other obstacles, but there were some trails at the stable. I took her out for lots of slow walks while her leg was healing." I looked at Russell hopefully. "Are there good places to ride around here?"

"You bet," he grinned. "I could show you how to get up on Sumas Mountain from here. There are lots of great trails up there."

"I'd love that!" I said, a little too eagerly. Then I blushed again – darn that Celtic complexion I had.

Russell gathered his reins and stepped up into the saddle. Sunny collected under him - eager to go - but waited, obedient to the rein. "Would you like to go for a ride tomorrow then?" Russell asked.

I drew in my breath, my heart racing. *Would I?*

"Uh...sure.... that would be great. What time?"

"I'll come after chores, about ten thirty, okay?"

"Sounds great. Thanks. See you tomorrow."

Russell touched his hand to the brim of his leather hat, nodded at me, and then with some invisible cue to Sundance, jumped the horse into a lope from a standstill and disappeared in a cloud of dust down the laneway and out onto the road.

CHAPTER TWO

I'm sure I drove my mom crazy all the rest of that day and again the next morning at breakfast. All I could talk about was Russell, his fabulous horse, and the fact that he was taking me riding.

I hadn't slept much, but was too wired to notice. I was up early and down to the barn to groom and put the English saddle on Redwing for our day's adventure.

This time, Buckwheat was paying attention, and he barked furiously as Russell and Sunny and a mostly- black Border Collie came trotting into the yard at precisely ten thirty. Gypsy rushed over to investigate Buckwheat, and after the mandatory posturing and butt sniffing, the two dogs began to play. I was holding Redwing by the bridle reins while she grazed the lush grass on the lawn but at Sunny's approach she lifted her head and whinnied loudly. He whinnied a greeting back and the two horses stood sniffing each other cautiously. Suddenly, Red squealed and struck out with a front foot, ears laced back and teeth bared. Quickly, I backed her up, and apologized. Russell just grinned and said, "It's okay, she's a girl." I wasn't sure what to think about that remark, so I let it go. I didn't want to get into an argument about the sexes.

I got a good look at the Livingston's dairy farm as we rode through it to get to the trails. They had a total of sixty acres of pasture, and some of the dry cows were up on leased land on the mountain. We were going to check on them on our ride. Russell's house, which was painted a pale yellow with brown trim, was a lot larger than our little white stucco bungalow. It had a large bay window at the front, which he told me was the living room. There were three dormer windows on the upper floor, and a large veranda with wide steps leading down to a pretty yard shaded by Weeping Willow and Mountain Ash trees. Past the house were the barns and pens that held the herd of eighty -some Holstein dairy cows. There was also a large metal clad machine shed and several other smaller shelters and outbuildings. These were for the calves and young stock that were not in the milking herd.

We rode through several pastures, with Russell and Sunny expertly opening and closing the gates without Russell having to get off. I admired the way he could side pass his horse up to the fence, lean over and open those gates, hold them open for Redwing and I to pass through, and then step sideways to close them again. I hadn't got so far with my mare's training to get her to respond to leg aids that well. On the racetrack with a small jockey perched almost on top of the withers, the horses worked entirely off the bridle and were not used to having a riders legs wrapped around their bellies. I was starting to get results with the lateral work I was doing with Red in the arena, but we had a long way to go to become the kind of team that Russell and Sunny were. I couldn't take my eyes off them.

Behind the farm the last gate opened onto an old road allowance that was grass covered and soft to the horses' feet. About a mile further on, we came to a small stream which Red had to make a fuss about crossing, and then the road petered out into a narrow trail that led into the woods and on up a steady incline to the hills and contours of Sumas Mountain.

After about an hour's climb, the trail evened out and disappeared in a beautiful grassy meadow. Russell said we should start to look for the cows. He also wanted to check if they needed any salt or minerals.

In ones and twos, and small bunches, we located the cattle which were browsing in the mountain meadows. Some were lying down, chewing their cuds happily in the shade of the big pine trees. I don't think Red had ever seen cows up close and personal like this. She didn't spook, but she craned her long neck to look at them and snorted in mock alarm as she came near them. When they lumbered to their feet, she stopped and stared, refusing to move forward. As she got used to seeing them, Sunny gave her confidence as he moved easily among the black and white bodies, and soon she relaxed and followed him happily.

When Russell was satisfied that all the cows were accounted for, he dismounted and slipped Sunny's bridle off. He clipped a pair of light chain hobbles around his front feet and left him to nibble on the grass. Then he moved over to a large flat rock that had been left in the meadow by the last ice age. "Come on over here, and have some lunch," he invited.

Feeling like a dork, I said, "What should I do with Red? I can't tie her up and I don't have hobbles." Another thing about racehorses is that someone at the track – a hotwalker, a groom, or a trainer, always holds them. They never seem to get tied up for any reason, and Red was no exception. I could now tie her in the barn where she was comfortable, but out here in strange territory, I wouldn't dare try it. She might pull back, break her lead- rope and gallop all the way home, or God knows where.

Russell took a bite of his sandwich, and then there was one of those silences while he chewed. Then he laid down his lunch and went over to Sunny. He removed his lariat from the off side of the saddle, came over to where I was holding Red by the bridle, and slipped the loop around her neck. "Okay," he said, take her bridle off and hold the end of this rope. She can eat and so can you. Problem solved."

"Thank-you," I grinned. "I can see I have some trail training to do to keep up to you."

I sat beside Russell on the big rock, holding the rope in one hand, and took my apple and granola bar out of my fanny pack that was strapped around my waist. I wondered if you could get saddlebags to attach to an English saddle. It would be much easier to have your horse carry your lunch.

We didn't talk much, but I found just being with Russell was easy. When we finished our lunch, he took the end of the rope that was attached to Redwing's neck, walked over to Sunny, and looped it around the saddle horn. "What are you doing?" I asked.

"I want to show you something, and the horses can't come," he said, with a smile. "I don't think she will leave Sunny, but if she tries to go, he is trained for calf roping, and if that rope tightens, he'll turn and face her and hold her."

"No kidding!" I said. I was suitably impressed. "Do you practice roping your dairy cows?"

"Uh...no, not usually...my dad would kill me if I fuzzed up his precious cows. I belong to High School Rodeo. There's a couple of us go to roping practice at one of the arenas on Thursday nights. It's great training for the horses, and it's a lot of fun." Russell spoke over his shoulder as he led the way up a narrow trail at the edge of the meadow. "You should come and watch sometime." "Thanks, I'd like that." I puffed. The hill was steep. I wasn't really into rodeo sports, being more interested in dressage and jumping, but anything to do with horses was okay by me, and if there was a certain young man involved, that made it all the more intriguing.

As we came out of the trees into a little clearing, a beautiful panoramic vista opened up to our view. Russell pointed to the south where a vast checkerboard of fields and farmland stretched as far as I could see. "That's the Sumas Prairie," he said. It stretches right down into the United States. Some of the best farmland you'll ever see." Then turning to the north, he continued, "That ribbon of blue down there, that's the Fraser River of course, and up on those dark hills over there, that's the Mission Monastery. You can just see the spires of the church."

"Oh wow," I said. "You mean there are monks living there, just like in Tibet?" He laughed. "Nah. I don't think they're Tibetan. More like an order of the Jesuits or something. I think they're Catholics. You can go and visit. I went with a school group a couple of years ago. They are totally self-supporting. They raise sheep, cows, pigs, grain, and fruit; everything they need. They have orchards, a flourmill, a forge," - "And a winery, I'll bet"- I interrupted.

Russell grinned again. "Yeah, I guess. They must have their wine for communion."

We made our way back down the narrow trail and bridled the horses. I had the feeling that I was quite privileged to be here in Russell's favorite place, alone with him.

When we got back down to the road allowance at the bottom of the mountain, Russell said, "Is Redwing hard to stop when she gets galloping?"

I replied, "Not unless there's a horse in front of her."

He said, "I'd sure like to see that horse run. Are you game for a little race?"

"You're on!" I grinned, already shortening my reins, and leaning forward over Red's withers. "You start, and we'll probably catch up to you."

Russell needed no encouragement, and neither did Sunny. Those two just seemed to instantly communicate. At a touch from Russell's heels, Sunny exploded into action. His golden rump was all we saw as he leaped away from us in a blistering gallop.

It took Red a couple of seconds to realize that we were in a race. I couldn't have held her back if I wanted to, and she plunged after Sunny in an explosive jump that must have covered all of twenty feet. Nearly unseated, I took a firm hold on the reins, braced my feet in the stirrups and felt the rush of adrenaline flow over my body as Red lined out and settled into her huge ground covering stride. The two dogs did their best to keep up.

Sunny was as fast as greased lightning, and he was already a quarter of a mile ahead of us, but as Russell turned to look over his shoulder, he was clearly astounded to see my big red horse gaining steadily on him.

Our riding styles were so different. Russell rode upright in his western saddle. His long legs hung down, making light contact with his horse's sides. He held the reins loosely in his left hand while Sunny pounded down the dirt track. I rode with a rein in each hand, almost standing in the stirrups of my English saddle in a three-point position, with strong contact on Red's mouth. In fact, my arms were almost falling off with the exertion of holding her at this tremendous pace. As Redwing flattened herself and stretched out even more, she caught up to and surged past Sundance in a blur of motion. With the wind whipping my eyes to tears I could barely see, but I sensed the change in her speed as she slowed slightly. She knew her job was done. I eased off on the reins, sat back in the saddle and spoke to her. "Easy Red, slow down now girl." My face was flushed and my eyes sparkled with the excitement of the chase. I knew I would never need drugs to get high as long as I had a horse like this. What a rush!

I held Red to a slow canter and then a long trot as Russell and Sundance came loping up beside us. We both dropped to a walk. "Well, that pony can drift," he said, with admiration in his voice. "And," he added, "You're quite a rider."

"Thanks," I replied modestly. "You guys are no slouches, either. That little horse can really travel. And you.... you just sit there so calm and relaxed.... like you were just going to light up a smoke or something. You're cool...just like the Marlboro Man." For once, it was Russell that blushed. Clearly, he liked the compliment.

CHAPTER THREE

My mom, Jean Wakefield, had managed
to get our five-acre parcel with a small
house, riding ring and barn for a lot less
than the advertised price. That was a
good thing, because we didn't have much
money. The catch was that it had stood
empty for some time after the old man
that had lived there passed away. The
grounds had a neglected, run-down look,
and the house smelled of male cats that
had come in through a broken window
and used the house for a shelter and
probably their wild orgies. The real estate
agent was actually kind of embarrassed
to show it, but immediately I saw its
charm and rustic beauty through the
junk, the jungle of overgrowth, and the
lack of upkeep. It had once been a part
of another dairy farm, and still had the
original hip-roofed barn with cattle
stanchions, a huge hayloft, and a shed
row with box stalls and a feed room.
When I saw that barn, I just had to have
the place. Mom wasn't impressed, but
when I promised to work my butt off
fixing up the property, she relented. It
was within our limited budget, and she
knew how badly I wanted a place of our
own so that I could look after Redwing
myself, and pursue a career involving
horses.

Mom was a registered nurse. She had worked in a medical clinic in Vancouver ever since my dad left us ten years ago, but for my sake, she agreed to leave her job in the city and look for work in Abbotsford, a much smaller center. She couldn't get on at the hospital, but was able to find a job at a nursing home called The Kanaka Lodge. It would do for a start, and we were both excited and a little scared of the new challenges that faced us.

Although we were not officially dating, Russell and I spent a lot of time together. Our friendship grew as the summer drew to a close. He was often over at our place helping with something or another, and our two families visited back and forth frequently and freely. Russell helped me to build some cavaletti and jumps for schooling Redwing. Together we painted the riding ring fence and the outside of the house a glistening white, and tackled the overgrown garden plot so that it could be used next spring. We took loads of old junk to the dump in Russell's beat up 1974 Ford pickup.

It didn't seem to matter what job my mom and I were working on; he was always willing and even eager to help. By the time school started, we had made a big difference to the appearance of our little acreage. It no longer looked derelict and sad. The lawn was cut, that wild lilac hedge was trimmed back, and the flowerbeds were cleaned out and replanted. We scrubbed the inside of the house until the nasty smells were gone. We scraped and painted all the walls. And because we had got the place cheaper than we had expected, Mom scrounged up some extra money from somewhere and bought new bathroom fixtures, and a new rug for the living room. It was still an old house, but it now was cozy, clean, and bright.

Ying-Yang supervised all our jobs, both indoors and out, keeping us entertained with her crazy antics. Gypsy always came with Russell, so the two dogs had a great time chasing each other around and snoozing on the lawn when they got tired.

When the work was all done, we celebrated with a house warming/picnic out in our newly tidied up back yard. Marcie and Ben, Russell's parents came, bringing a huge roasting pan full of delicious barbequed beef ribs. Everyone brought something totally yummy, either a salad or dessert. My oldest grown-up married sister, Maryanne arrived with her husband Dave, and their two kids, five-year-old Jessie and seven year old Luke. My other sister, Sarah, was married to a research chemist, and they were presently living in Atlanta, Georgia where Steven worked at the university, so of course, they couldn't come. No one mentioned my dad, or what a hard struggle it had been for Mom to raise us girls without him. Some part of me still missed him, because I couldn't ever remember him being unkind to me, but I guess it was a different story for Mom. Some day, I would have to ask her what really happened, but for now it was a closed subject.

The week before school started, Russell drove me to Abbey High for registration. The school counselors welcomed me, and gave me a tour of the school. It sure was a lot smaller than Kitsilano. I felt a little bit sad as I realized I wouldn't be graduating with the friends I had made in the last years of highschool, but Russell made up for all of that. We were both on the academic program, so we would be taking most of the same courses and would be in the same classes. As we drove home he said, "You'll be riding the school bus with me. I get on before you, so I'll save you a seat. Mrs. Klein is our driver and she's pretty cool. She lets us high school kids sit wherever we want as long as we obey the bus rules and keep the noise down. Just don't drop any garbage on her floor, and don't bop from seat to seat, or she'll yell at you. She's pretty strict about the rules. We're on for about forty minutes, so it's not too bad. I'll be driving sometimes too, so I can pick you up on those days. If you want." he added.

"Of course", I agreed. " I'd like that." So far, I hadn't got tired of being in Russell's company, and he seemed to like being with me too.

When September rolled around, school started, Mom started her new job, and we settled into a kind of new routine. I didn't get involved in any extra-curricular activities like basketball or drama club, because all I wanted to do in my spare time was ride. Russell wanted me to join his High School Rodeo Club and train Redwing for barrel racing, but I wasn't interested in that. I didn't want to run her all the time, even though she would have been good at it. I was interested in learning more about training hunter/jumper horses and in doing the conditioning dressage levels that made for a collected, balanced, supple athlete. So every Saturday, unless the weather was too awful, I rode Redwing down our quiet country roads to English riding lessons with Pam Arthur at the Eagle Ridge Equestrian Center. To pay for these lessons, and to get a little extra money, I also worked at the stable every day after school from four to six p.m. The stalls had been cleaned by the morning shift,

so my job was to shake out the bedding,
scrub and fill the water buckets, put the
flakes of hay into the mangers and dole
out the grain into the feed tubs. Then, I
would bring the horses in that had been
turned out for the day and put them into
their stalls for the night. If the weather
had been too nasty that day, and the
horses hadn't been turned out, I had to
pick up the manure in the stalls with the
pitchfork, and add some fresh bedding.

I loved this job; loved the sounds
and the smells of the horses; loved the
way they greeted me with their little
snorts and whinnies when I brought their
food and came to get them to come in for
the night. Most of the animals were of the
hunter type, although not necessarily
Thoroughbreds like Redwing. There were
some Anglo-Arabs, a couple of
Appaloosas, and a selection of ponies
that belonged to members of the Otter
Road Pony Club. Most were being trained
for, or being used for jumping. Usually I
walked the two miles home, which I
didn't mind as long as it wasn't raining
too hard. Mom couldn't pick me up, as
she worked a twelve-hour shift at the
Lodge and was never around when I
needed a ride home. Russell kept offering
to come and get me, but for a long time I
held out, not wanting to be a bother. I
would pull my long yellow rain slicker

over my coat, don a toque and gloves and
head out into the dark, wind, and rain.

CHAPTER FOUR

The first time Russell kissed me was on one of those dark, rainy, windy nights in December. I had stepped out of the coziness of the barn into a really nasty night to find him waiting for me in his battered old blue truck. "Boy, am I glad to see you!" I said as I slid into the warmth of the truck cab.

"Why don't you call me when it's wild like this?" he answered, reproach in his voice. "I told you I don't mind coming for you. I hate to think of you walking home in the dark and the rain."

"Oh," I teased, "I didn't realize you were thinking of me all that much."

He gave me a look that was part scorn, part concern as the old truck bumped over the potholes in the barnyard and lurched out onto the road. I was treated to one of his lapses of silence as he concentrated on driving with the heavy rain slashing sideways against the windshield.

We pulled up into my darkened yard. Russell knew I still had to go down to the barn to feed Redwing, and that I had to make my own supper. "Would you like some help?" he asked, hopefully.

"No thanks, I'll be fine," I said. "Thanks a lot for the ride." I started to open the truck door. Buck was bouncing up and down outside, frantic to greet me.

28

"Lindz," he said...I waited.

"What?"

"Uh...would you go to the Christmas dance with me?" I took my hand off the door handle and turned back to him.

"Well yeah, we're all going, aren't we? " I was referring to the group of kids that we always hung out with at school.

Russell kind of squirmed in his seat. Then he tried again. I just hadn't got it the first time. "Yes, but I was wondering...if you would...you know... go with me as my date."

It dawned on me then, that our relationship was finally moving up to a new level. I felt a thrill of excitement.

I looked out at Buckwheat's puzzled face. He was trying to figure out why I wasn't getting out of the truck. I couldn't help but grin. Then I looked into Russell's dark eyes and said, "I would like that very much."

We moved together then, somewhat awkwardly, and he put his arm around my shoulders. "Can I kiss you?" he asked.

A smile tugged at the corners of my mouth. "I think that under the circumstances that would be entirely okay.... and nice," I added. To myself I thought *it's about time!* I guess in 1984 it still wasn't proper for a girl to ask a guy out, or make the first move. In any case, I had been waiting a long time for this. His kiss was everything I had hoped it would be – long, and gentle and sweet. I had had a boyfriend last year in grade eleven. His name was Bill Brennan, and he was always trying to kiss me. His lips were thin and hard, and when we kissed, it hurt. Once our teeth gnashed together, and it gave me the creeps, like someone scratching the blackboard with their fingernails. Bill was nice, but he became a pest and he wanted more than kissing, so I let him know it was over. I was glad Russell and I had got to be such good friends first, but I was ready for a little romance with him.

We kissed a couple more times and then he just held me tight, breathing softly into my ear. I hated to get out of the truck and face the rain, but I had to get going. "Goodnight," I whispered against his cheek. "Thanks for rescuing me."

"See you in the morning" he said, as he leaned over me and opened the truck door, planting another little kiss on my lips as he did so.

After that night, we kissed a lot. Russell started picking me up in the mornings for school, and he was always there at the arena to drive me home. We kissed hello and we kissed goodbye, and we kissed in the hallway at our lockers when we met for lunch. We held hands and cuddled when we studied or watched T.V. but it didn't go any farther. Oh, we talked about it plenty. We talked about everything. We'd been to parties where a couple would disappear behind closed doors. We weren't that dumb to not realize what was going on. Some of our friends were sexually active, but they didn't seem to be any happier than we were with each other, and I was glad when Russell said, "Let's wait."

Christmas came and went. Russell looked after our animals while Mom and I went to spend a few days with Maryanne and Dave and the kids in Vancouver.

A few days before we left, Russell drove into the yard with a mysterious looking box in the back of the truck, along with some lumber and wire. "Get in", he said when I came out to meet him. We drove through the gate and across the pasture to our big barn. He went around to the back of the truck and lifted out the box. It had air holes punched in it, and I suspected there was an animal of some kind in it. "Merry Christmas!" he grinned. "It's not a very romantic kind of a present, but, knowing you, I think you'll like it."

He set the box on the ground. Gently, I pulled open the flaps of the box, and there, nestled in the shavings, were six little brown bantam hens and a

31

golden rooster. I picked one up and held her under my chin. "Oh, they're just a perfect gift! I love them!" I said. I put the hen back and closed the flaps so they wouldn't fly out. I turned to Russell and gave him a big hug and a kiss. "You must have overheard me telling Mom I wanted to get some chickens," I said.

"Yeah," he laughed. "Several times." Then he added. "Well, let's get to work. These chickens need a pen and some nest boxes.

For the next two hours we happily worked together, closing in one of the old box stalls with chicken wire, and building a row of nesting boxes, and a roost. I went up to the house and found some old pans that would do for their water and grain. Russell had thought of that too. What I thought were bags of horse feed in the back of the truck, turned out to be wheat and laying meal for my birds. Russell had thought of everything. The bantams were tipped out of the box into their new home where they immediately started scratching, singing, eating, crowing and checking out the nest boxes. I knew I would enjoy having them in the barn, and looked forward to having fresh eggs every day too.

CHAPTER FIVE

Unlike other parts of Canada, spring comes early in the Fraser Valley. The grass stays green all year round, and by March the Lily of the Valley, Crocuses, and Hyacinths were all poking their noses out of the soggy soil.

I had worked hard to get Redwing ready for the Spring Schooling Show to be held on the second Sunday at the Chilliwack Equestrian Center. As one of Pam's students, I was going with a group of other riders. The horses were being transported in a large van that belonged to the stable.

I rode Redwing down on Saturday, and instead of having a lesson, I put her into the wash stall and gave her a bath. Lots of horses put up a real fuss at getting wet, and having the water squirt at them from the hose. But not Red. She loved the water, letting me run the hose over her face. She even drank out of the hose. There were certain advantages to having a racetrack-trained horse. She sure wasn't afraid of much.

After her bath, I stood on a box in her stall and pulled her mane with a small metal comb until it was nice and short and even. For jumping classes, a long, full mane just got in the way of your hands and reins, so it was standard procedure to keep the mane short. I also banded her mane. That involved wrapping little colored elastics around a section of mane hairs close to the neckline so that it would lay down flat. After that I groomed her hard, to bring the natural oil back into her coat, and sprayed her with Super Shine. Then I painted her hooves with Hoof Black. I had more beauty aides in my tack box than I had for myself at home. I covered her with a light summer sheet to keep her clean and left her in her rented stall with hay and water for the night.

Our first show went pretty well. I entered Red in four classes; English Pleasure, English Equitation, Baby Green Hunter, where the jumps were only 2'6", and in Dressage, Training Level Test 1. Dressage was first, and I was nervous. I had memorized the pattern and practiced it many times, but I was sure I would forget it once I was out in that ring performing alone in front of an audience. Some of that nervousness passed through my body to Redwing, as she didn't do quite as well as I had expected. She didn't like the collected work and she fussed a little at being held in - fussiness that manifested itself in her chewing on the bit and swishing her tail. Those were minor disobediences but we were marked down for them. Out of eight entries we placed fourth. Afterwards, the Judge talked to each competitor, and discussed his or her scores, helping each of us to see where we needed improvement. The judge complimented me on my lovely mare, and mentioned that her impulsion, or desire to move forward was wonderful, but it needed to be contained somewhat; that her elasticity of steps and engagement of hindquarters was good. What needed work was Red's acceptance of the bit, the correctness of her lateral bends, and her attention and confidence. These things, I knew, would improve each time out.

She did improve quite a lot for the flat classes. We placed in both – got a fourth and a fifth, but the classes were large and I was happy with her performance.

Jumping was more to Red's liking than the discipline of the dressage arena. We were both more relaxed and went out there just to have fun. I pretended we were just in our old arena at home, going over the practice jumps. Clearing the jumps was no problem for Redwing, and she had a clear round. She could have easily jumped twice as high, but what the judge wanted to see was a consistent rhythm, the proper number of strides between the jumps, clean changes of leads; suppleness and balance between horse and rider and no refusals, of course. We must have done a fairly decent job, because we came away with a second place ribbon!

Russell had picked Mom up after his morning milking chores and they had arrived in time to watch my classes. We were finished by noon, but there was more advanced dressage and jumping all afternoon. Although I was immersed in watching each class to learn all that I could, Russell and Mom were getting bored watching the same old stuff over and over again. Red was being transported home in the van at the end of the day, so at Russell's suggestion, he took us out to supper on the way home.

That first show was only the beginning. I knew I had to find a way to make a living with riding, training, and breeding horses. It was in my blood.

Later that week I cornered Pam, my riding instructor, and asked her how I should go about studying horsemanship in a serious way. I could go a long way with Pam, as she had been short listed for the Canadian Olympics in show jumping, but I could not afford years of lessons, or the expensive horses that were required to compete internationally. Besides, I was graduating in a few months, and I needed to earn a living.

Pam said, "Come on into my office. I think I can give you some information that will help you." I followed her into her inner sanctuary- a small, messy room next to the tack room. There was an old couch with a couple of barn cats sleeping on it, a desk covered with papers and horse journals, shelves lined with horse books and binders. The room smelled of leather, stale cigarette smoke, and horses. I moved one of the cats and sat down while Pam rifled through some papers on her desk. She pulled out a magazine and then selected one of the loose-leaf binders from the shelf. She lit up a cigarette and sat down at her desk.

" You and your horse are showing a lot of talent," she began. "You've both improved tremendously since you started here."

"I've got a great teacher," I said. "You've given us a lot of help." Pam grinned. "Thanks." Then she continued. "I'm going to be blunt. This sport takes money -lots of money to get anywhere. Most of my students come from rich families...you know... their daddies are big wheel executives. They have connections and corporate sponsors and the like." She looked at me pointedly, taking a drag on her cigarette.

"I know what you're getting at," I said. We're not rich, and I know I won't be able to compete in this game. What I would like though, is to learn how to raise and train horses, and run a breeding farm. I need to learn the business end of running a stable. Where can I learn how to succeed in the horse industry?"

"Okay, that's what I needed to know," Pam smiled. " I think I can help you." I leaned forward with interest.

"I get a lot of horse magazines," she said. I nodded. That was obvious from the clutter everywhere. "And," she continued, "in these wonderful magazines, are sometimes ads for big breeding establishments looking for working students. You work for them and they give you some riding instruction and teach you what you need to know to run your own place. There's a great place that I know of in Virginia, called Linden Hall Equestrian Center. I trained there one winter when we were preparing for the Olympics. I'll give you the address and you can contact them to see if they will accept any students. You can take home a bunch of these World of Dressage magazines. You might find something in the ads that suits you. If you do, let me know, and I'll write you a good reference letter."

"Thanks a lot, Pam." I gushed. "That's a wonderful help." Then I asked her, "Where did you get your training and experience with horses?"

Pam ground out her cigarette in the ashtray. Thank goodness. The smell was almost gagging me. She handed me a stack of magazines, and sat back in her chair. "Oh, I'm from England, you know. I came up through the ranks of Pony Club in Somerset. I learned to stick on a horse over jumps while riding with the local hunt club."

"That must have been a blast, riding to hounds," I said. "I'd love to do that."

"Yes," she agreed, "it's very exciting." Her gray eyes took on a far-a-way look, like she was remembering those days.

"Were your parents wealthy?" I asked her, hoping I wasn't being too inquisitive.

"We were fairly well off. My dad indulged all of us and encouraged us to follow our dreams. Mine was to ride, so he sent me over to Germany when I was seventeen to study horsemanship with a top trainer. I got a lot of chances to compete and ride top horses over there. It's a different world. Everything is so old and established and there is state money supporting the international show jumpers. Over here, its very hard to get financial support." Pam sat up and looked at me intently. "Would you be interested in going to England?"

I looked back just as intently at her. It was an idea that had not occurred to me. "Um...I hadn't thought of it.... why?"

"Well...I have connections there that I could refer you to, and the British Horse Society has a program that starts you out as a groom and then teaches you everything about breeding and foaling, nutrition, accounting and office skills, and of course riding. You get a certificate at the end of the course. It's an excellent program, and I know that B.H.S. graduates are in demand all over the world."

I couldn't believe my ears! This was exactly what I had been looking for! But in England? It was so far away from home – from Mom, from Russell, from Redwing, everything I loved. I wasn't sure if I could handle it.

Pam stood and turned to her bookshelf. She pulled out a thick pamphlet and handed it to me. "Here's some information on the B.H.S. and a list of farms that take working pupils. Go home and do some research and get back to me with what you decide."

I stood to leave. My head was spinning with new thoughts and ideas. "Thanks, Pam." I said. "I have some serious reading and decision making to do."

"Good luck," she said with a grin. "Once you've got this horse disease, you never fully recover."

CHAPTER SIX

For the next couple of nights after work, chores, and homework, I poured over the horse magazines, and the material from the B.H.S. There were all kinds of opportunities, but I was in a real dither about which direction to go in, and I knew I would have a hard time convincing Russell that I needed to go away for training. When I had mentioned it to him, he got real quiet and I knew he was upset.

As soon as Mom got home from work, we sat down to the supper I had prepared. I showed her the ads I had circled. I narrowed it down to several training stables in the U.S. that would take working students. Mom was skeptical.

"Well Lindsey," she said, "You know that I think a career with horses will only give you a life of drudgery. Surely you don't want to be mucking stalls all your life."

"No Mom," I said, rolling my eyes heavenward. "The horse industry is growing by leaps and bounds. I want to be a part of it. I want to teach riding, and raise good horses. I want to learn breeding management and how to do basic vet work and foot care and...and...oh... there's just so much to it. It's all I've ever wanted to do. You know I live and breathe horses.

"Yes, I know...and God knows where that gene came from." She took the magazine I was holding out and looked at the circled want ad. It was for Kenridge Farm in Stanton, Kentucky. They were a show stable with Morgans and Saddlebred horses, and they advertised breeding, showing, training, and sales.

"Kentucky!" Mom said, raising her eyebrows.

"Yeah, I've always wanted to see the blue grass of Kentucky." I said. "There are so many big horse farms there. It would be great to work on one of them." I shoved another article under Mom's nose. "And here's the one that Pam trained at. It's in Virginia. It's called Linden Hall, and it's very famous. The American Olympic Team trains there." I pointed at the accompanying pictures of fancy barns, white board fences, and expensive looking horses. "I would love to go there and take lessons from the nation's top riders."

"Well," Mom said, "I suppose it wouldn't hurt to write and ask them what kind of a deal they offer. I'm just afraid you would be doing all the grunge labor and getting very little in return for it. You would have no one to turn to if they took advantage of you. You would have to make certain you had a valid contract with the working conditions and amount of instruction spelled out on it."

This had not occurred to me, but now that Mom mentioned it, I could see it was a definite possibility. "Yeah, I guess you're right." I agreed. Then I brought up the B.H.S. idea.

"Mom," I ventured. I was sure this idea would be shot down in flames. "There's another possibility, but it's in England." I saw the startled look cross her face, and then she blurted out, "Your dad's in England."

"What?" I said. I was astonished! "Why didn't you ever tell me where he was? "

Mom sighed. "I guess I should have, but I just didn't want to worry and upset you. I thought it best if you forgot about him. I know I try to."

My eyes filled with tears. "I guess I *am* still mad at him for leaving us. "What happened with you two, Mom? Why did he leave? How could he have done that to you...to us?"

Mom's pretty gray-green eyes were misty too. Her permed hair was almost all gray now, as it curled around her face. She was still pretty. I couldn't understand why Dad had left her so long ago with three girls to raise. She must have been burned pretty badly not to marry again. She never even had a boyfriend over the years that I knew of. I waited for an answer.

Mom shrugged her shoulders and poured tea into her cup. "Tea?" she asked. I held out my cup.

"Your dad is English, you know, from a little village called Seahouses in Northumberland. He always wanted to go back there but I never thought he was serious about it. I had my nursing career, and was making good money, and I didn't want to leave Canada. He was lots of fun. We had a crazy courtship, and it wasn't that serious, but then I found out that Maryanne was on the way. So we got married. Then Sarah came along and then you. I found out after a while that he was still corresponding with an old flame in England that he had gone to school with. Eventually, he just left to go home and be with her."

"Oh, my God." I said. I reached out and covered Mom's hand with mine. I felt so awful for her. What a devastating thing to be abandoned like that.

"Did he ever send you any money, or send anything for us kids?" I asked. I could not remember ever getting a present from my father.

"Oh yes," Mom said. "I was a fool, and never asked for anything. Too proud, I guess. He would send money for your birthdays, so most of the things that were

44

from me were from him as well. I just never told you so."

We sat lost in our thoughts for a little while. Then Mom said, "Russell loves you. It's going to break his heart if you go away."

I looked into Mom's eyes. "I know...and I love him...I think – Oh God, how do you really know for sure? I think I'm scared because of what happened to you. Russell's my first serious boyfriend. How can I be sure he's the one for me?"

Mom just smiled. You'll know. The best thing about your relationship is that you started out as good friends. That's what it will come back to once all the passion and excitement has died."

"Does it have to die?" I asked.

"It takes a lot of work to keep the sparks flying, especially once the babies come along and the bills mount up, and there's sickness and job worries to deal with. We never know what curves life is going to throw at us, but if your partner is a good friend, and you can talk things out, then you have a good chance of making it together." Mom got up from the table and started gathering the dishes. "Russell's a fine boy," she said. Then out of the blue, she looked over her shoulder at me and asked, "Are you sleeping with him?"

"No!" I blushed at least ten shades of scarlet and buried my head in my hands.

"Well, I'm sorry for asking," she said, all businesslike. "I just don't want you to get caught. If you're considering it, please get yourself on contraceptives first."

"Yes, Mom," I mumbled. We were quiet for a moment while she busied herself with washing the dishes. I got up to put the food away and dry the dishes.

"Well, what about this British riding thing" Mom asked. "We kind of got sidetracked there for a while."

I breathed a sigh of relief that the previous subject was closed. Then I proceeded to tell her about the B.H.S. program with it's training in business management as well as horsemanship. To my surprise, she asked for all the literature that Pam had given me, and went to sit in the living room to read it. I was on pins and needles until she finished. Then she said, "You know, this looks like a good program. It has National standards, and they cover all aspects of a breeding and training operation. I see that there is classroom instruction in typing and bookkeeping, and office procedures. It's just like a school with exams in both written and practical work. You get a small salary for your work, plus your room and board. The stables are government inspected several times a year and there is a board of governors for grievances, such as if you don't receive your pay, or you are mistreated in any way. You get a diploma at the end of your training, and there's a job placement program. I think you should look into this."

"Are you serious, Mom? You'd really let me go?" I was finding her interest hard to believe. "I'd have to save up my fare to get over there." I added.

"Well, I've been putting part of the family allowance aside for you for the past ten years." Mom said. I was flabbergasted. I'd had no idea. "There's about two thousand dollars. You can have it to go to England, if that's what you really want."

I wasn't usually very demonstrative with my mom, but I flung myself into her arms and hugged her tight. "Oh Mom! Thanks so much!" I cried. "This is so exciting!"

I ran to my room to compose a letter of application, and made a mental note to ask Pam for a reference tomorrow.

CHAPTER SEVEN

In a few days, I mailed off my letter to England, and also three to riding establishments in the United States. During Easter holidays, Russell and I rode up to the meadows on Sumas Mountain, and I tried to talk to him about my plans.

We were sitting on the rock where we usually ate our lunch and talked about the things that were important to us. It was hard to discuss things while riding. Russell had made me a pair of chain hobbles like he had for Sunny, and I had trained Redwing to tolerate having her front feet tied together. I don't think she would have left Sunny anyway, but it was nice to let the two horses graze without worrying about them taking off while we lazed around in the spring sunshine.

Russell took my hand and said, "Lindsey, I can't understand why you want to go away. You can get all the training you want right here. You can go to Business College and learn all that office stuff, and there are plenty of good trainers right here in the Valley. I can teach you to ride western, and you could keep on with your English lessons at Eagle Ridge."

I sighed. "Yeah, I know.... but there are no *certified* programs here like the one in England. Besides, I want to have a little adventure in my life before I settle down. I've never been anywhere."

Russell moved off the rock over to a grassy knoll and sat down on the ground, being careful to check for cow patties first. He patted the space beside him, and invited. "Come here."

He reached for me as I lowered myself beside him, and he pulled me into a close embrace. Our bodies were touching all the way down as he kissed me several times. It felt heavenly, being so close to him, and I thought for a fleeting moment that all I wanted was to be with him, now and forever.

He smiled into my eyes. "What are you thinking now? I held him tight and closed my eyes.

"I'm thinking I want you more than I should." I replied honestly.

Russell propped himself up on one elbow. He stroked my hair and face gently with his fingers. "Lindz"...he said softly. "Let's just get married. I love you. I can't bear to let you go. He kissed me again, deeper and more urgent then. We clung to each other, trying hard to resist the urges that were sweeping over us. I broke away first, and rolled away from him.

I sat with my back to him, and looked out over the valley. "I love you too Russell," I said, "But I'm scared. I don't think I'm ready for marriage yet."

I heard the pleading in his voice as he said, "What are you scared of?"

I turned to face him. "I'm not sure. My parents' failed marriage for one thing. We haven't even dated anyone else. Not that I *want* to, but maybe we *should* before things go too far."

"Are you breaking up with me?" he asked.

"No! Of course not." I moved back into his arms and hugged him. "I just think we should give it some more time... even a year wouldn't hurt. That's why I think it's okay if I go away. If our love is real, it can wait."

I could tell Russell wasn't convinced, but for now, he accepted defeat.

We did lots of riding and exploring as the days grew longer and the rainy season relented. Russell helped me tear out the old saggy barbed wire fence at the back of our property and replace it with new wire. In the corner of our land, we installed a recycled metal gate that he got at the dump. This gave us access to the dykes and gravel bars along the river, and we rode for miles side by side with one hand in each other's, and the other on the reins. Once in a while we raced the horses, but mostly we rode at a walk. The two dogs were always with us, having all kinds of adventures following their noses as they crossed the pathways of waterfowl, foxes, and skunks. Buckwheat always loved to get wet. He'd flop down in any old ditch that held water, and when we rode near the river, he couldn't wait to get in for a swim. Gypsy, on the other hand, hated to get his beautiful coat wet. He'd go around the wet spots if he could and looked at Buck with sympathy whenever he immersed himself in the river.

 Our graduation ceremony was coming up soon and all the senior classes were abuzz with preparations. The grade elevens were doing the decorations, grad committees had been formed to arrange the banquet, the entertainment and the dance. Of course Russell asked me to go with him, and of course, I accepted.
I was in a quandary about what to wear. I didn't want to spend a fortune on a dress that I would never use again. That was all the girls in my group talked about – their dresses, where they were getting their hair done, what to wear for pictures, who had asked who to the dance, and so on.
My sister Maryanne came to my rescue. She had been a bridesmaid in a friend's wedding quite a few years back, and she still had the dress. I jumped at the chance to borrow it. She brought it out to the farm, and luckily for me, it fit me perfectly. It was a pale mauve color

with short sleeves, with the skirt descending in layers of taffeta and silk almost to the floor. I found some silver high heels at the local thrift store, and although I knew wearing them would be torture, I bought them.

On Graduation Day, none of us went to classes. My girlfriends, Jill and Sue picked me up and we all went to our appointments at the same hairdressers. Deb, my stylist, swept my long blonde hair onto the top of my head and secured it with elastic. Then she wet the long strands and rolled them up in fat rollers. These were then dried and combed out and the curls were pinned in a circle around my head. Deb placed a small tiara in the center of the curls, and then razor cut my bangs. It looked great! I had never worn my hair up, and I was surprised at how different and yes, even lovely I looked.

Russell must have thought so too. When he came to pick me up for the banquet, his face registered surprise and delight when he saw me in my gorgeous gown and tiara. He had never seen me wearing heels, white gloves, and makeup before. With clumsy hands, he pinned my pretty yellow orchid that he had brought me onto my dress. He kissed my cheek and whispered, "You look fabulous!"

He looked very handsome himself. I was not used to seeing him without his old leather cowboy hat and boots. He was resplendent in a black tuxedo, pink shirt, tie, cufflinks, and polished shoes.

A roast beef dinner was served to all the grads and guests in the gymnasium. I guess the organizers wanted to make sure we all had some food in our bellies before we hit the various parties and the drinks. During the meal, there were speeches and presentations, and then all of us girls traipsed out to the washrooms to repair our makeup before we donned the black gowns and caps to walk across the stage for the last time and get our diplomas. After that, the gym was cleared for the dance. My dance card was full, with the first and last being reserved for Russell.

By midnight I had kicked off the awful shoes and had had enough of being dressed like a princess. Russell drove me home so I could change into jeans and a sweater. Then I waited in his truck while he went in and got into his comfortable grunge clothes. We were going to an all-night party at Patricia Walls, one of the girls in our group.

The music was blaring; the booze was flowing. Russell had a couple of beers. I sipped on some wine. I really didn't like alcohol very much. We danced most of the night, fell asleep in each other arms on the couch for a while, then got up and danced some more. Some couples had disappeared into bedrooms and one guy was dancing on his knees with his face pressed against his girlfriend's stomach, and his hands on her butt. I knew where they were going to end up before the night was over.

George, a guy in my math class was there alone. George wore heavy glasses, and he wasn't very good looking. I knew he was getting drunk and feeling lonely. He came over when Russell had gone to the washroom and asked me for a dance. I said "okay" and we were having fun twirling around when Russell came back. I could see by his face that he wasn't happy about me dancing with someone else, but I thought *"What the heck – it's grad!"* Maybe George did hold me a little too close, and his hand did kind of slide down my backside once or twice, but I ignored it. That is, until Russell came over and tapped George on the shoulder.

"Hey man," he said, "That's my girl you're groping." His steely blue eyes bored into George's bleary ones. George dropped his hands and turned to face Russell.

"Well just get lost, asshole!" he said. "Me and the lady are just enjoying a dance." I backed away as I saw Russell flush with anger. His fist came up and smashed into George's belly. George crumpled and fell over, passed out.

Russell grabbed my hand, and said, "Come on, Lindsey, lets go."

"Wait!" I said. "Let's see if he's okay first." A small crowd had gathered around George. Patricia rolled him over and we all saw that he was breathing all right. He just needed to sleep. I think we all did. Two of the boys carried George to a couch and covered him with a blanket. That little episode kind of broke up the party, and we all said our goodnights and headed for home.

Russell apologized to me on the way home. He said, "I just don't know what came over me Linz. I get so jealous when other guys look at you. I just want you so much...please marry me?"

I kissed him goodnight and said, "We're much too tired to discuss this tonight... I mean this morning. Let's get some sleep."

CHAPTER EIGHT

The first week of June, with only three weeks of school left, I received a letter from England. Unfortunately, Russell was driving me home from the arena when I picked up the mail, and I couldn't conceal my excitement when I saw the blue envelope from overseas. I tucked it under some flyers, intending to read it at home.

"Go ahead and open it," Russell said, "You're just about busting out of your skin with excitement."

"Okay," I shrugged. I slit the edge of the thin blue letter and unfolded it. I read out loud.

'Dear Miss Wakefield,
Your application has been reviewed, and on the basis of your experience and interest, you have been approved for enrollment in our Working Student Program. The program has been designed to last for a year, with the next available opening being September 8th, 1985. You have been allocated to the Fulmer Equestrian Center, 10 Downs Road, Eastgate Gardens, Taunton, Somerset. Please telephone to Ms. Liz Bryant, Headmistress, as soon as possible to confirm your registration....

The letter went on to give me the telephone number and a few more details

56

but I skipped over them. I turned to Russell and said, "Oh God, Russell, what should I do? Should I go?" My hands were shaking, and my face was flushed.

His face showed no emotion as he looked at me steadily. "I think you've already made up your mind, haven't you? Isn't it what you want?"
I nodded, feeling miserable all of a sudden. I leaned over to kiss him goodbye, but he didn't kiss me back.

"At least we'll have the summer together," he grumbled. But it was not to be.

That very night, when Mom got home from work, I knew from her manner that she had something exciting to tell me. "Mom, what gives?" I asked her. "Have you got a boyfriend, or something?" I pestered. "You look positively secretive, but you're just bursting to tell me what it is!"

"Wait a minute, wait a minute!" she laughed, as she sat and removed her shoes, rubbing her sore feet. She hated dayshift. She was on her feet for twelve hours and it was exhausting work. She actually liked the nightshift better when most of the residents were sleeping. It was not nearly as demanding. And there was one old gal that had trouble sleeping and Mom would get to sit and read to her if she had time. The only bad thing about

the nightshift though, was that she had
to leave me alone at night. It was a
wonder Russell and I hadn't slept
together yet. We certainly had plenty of
opportunities.

"Well! Guess what?" Mom said,
jarring me back to my senses.

"What? I have no idea."
Mom came and sat at the kitchen table,
looking approvingly at the beef stew and
dumplings I set in front of her. She
picked up her fork and started to eat.

"You remember Mrs. Donnelly, that
little lady who has a bad hip?"

"Yeah, " I said, "The one that's such
an avid reader and talker?" I had been to
the lodge a few times, and had met most
of the patients at one time or another.

"The very one," Mom said. "She's
very wealthy, you know."

"Oh yeah?" I said. "So...is she
leaving you all her money in her will?"

"No," Mom said, "but it's almost as
good." She was mopping up the gravy
with her bread. "Mrs. Donnelly wants to
go on a trip overseas. She has relatives in
Scotland that she would like to see, and
she is going to book a cruise on the
H.M.R. S. Carinthia, out of Southampton.
She wants to spend the winter in a hotel
in Portugal, and then book passage on a
ship through the Panama Canal home to
Vancouver sometime next May."

"Well, that's wonderful," I said. "She might as well spend her money. She can't take it with her when she dies, and she's getting pretty old."

"You haven't guessed yet, have you?" Mom asked, her eyes sparkling.

"Um..no...what?"

"Well, she asked me if I would go with her, as her nurse/companion. No salary, but all expenses paid, of course."

"Oh wow, Mom! That's wonderful!" I said. "I hope you said 'yes!'"

Mom looked thoughtful. "I haven't yet. I wanted to talk to you first. I need to know where you're going to be. If you're going to be away, I'll need to stay to look after the place."

I looked at my mother in disbelief. "Mom, don't miss out on the chance of a lifetime! You've always wanted to go traveling. Look at all the books you read – they're all about going places and seeing the world. And even in your dreams you travel. You are always telling me about some exotic place you've been in your mind."

Mom smiled and nodded. "You're right Lindsey. Maybe I've been dreaming about the places I'm going to visit."

I went over to the desk in the corner of the kitchen and brought over the flimsy blue letter from England. "Look Mom," I said, "I've been accepted at a stable in Somerset. They want me there by September the 8th. I'd like to go."

Mom got up from the table and hugged me. "Let's both go, then," she said. "Let's both have an adventure!" We just held on to each other for a long minute, thinking of all the rapid changes that were swirling around us.

"When does Mrs. Donnelly want to go?" I asked, letting go of Mom and sitting back down at the kitchen table.

"I'm not sure, sometime this summer, I think".

"Well, why don't you go and phone her and find out? And tell her you'll go with her on her trip. We can figure out what to do with the place later." I didn't want Mom to lose out on this opportunity, and I don't think she did either, because she went to her bedroom to phone the Lodge.

So many thoughts whirled through my mind. I felt dizzy. The thought of leaving my animals brought tears to my eyes. *What about Redwing? Who would look after Buckwheat and Ying-Yang? We couldn't just leave the place empty for a year! Could Russell live in our place and look after it?*

Mom came back to the kitchen and said that she had talked to Mrs. Donnelly, and that the elderly lady was delighted that Mom had decided to go with her. She was going to go ahead and make the travel arrangements for the end of July. That was only seven weeks away!

Then Mom sprung another surprise on me. "Lindsey," she said. "Why don't you fly over to London with us, and come on a tour of England and Scotland before you go to your horse farm?" Mrs. Donnelly actually suggested it, and offered to pay for your expenses too."

"She did?" I was astounded. "Why would she do that? She hardly knows me!"

Mom looked thoughtful. "I'm not sure. She has grown children of her own, but they never come to visit, and I think there's some animosity there. She used to ride horses as a youngster back in Scotland, so I think she likes the fact that you are so horsy. I just think she's terribly lonely, and would enjoy the company. Money is no object for her. Her husband left her very well off." Mom looked at me searchingly. "Will you come?"

"Sure!" I grinned. "I would be stupid not to. I'll stop in at the Lodge tomorrow to thank her in person."

Mom smiled. "She'll love that. Bring her some pictures of you and Redwing. She 's so interested in your riding career. She'll be thrilled that you're going to England to study. Of course, it's not as good as Scotland, but at least it's the old county."

"So...now..." Mom said. "We have to move fast to get things organized. Do you think Russell would look after your pets?"

"I'm not sure," I replied hesitantly. "He's kind of mad at me. He's going to have a real hissy fit about me leaving so soon. He thought we'd at least have the summer together."

"Poor Russell," Mom sighed. "It's going to be hard for him to let you go."

"I know," I said. "It's hard for me too. But if I stay here, I know he's going to pressure me to get married, and I don't want to. Not yet."

Mom nodded in agreement. "Well, I suppose Maryanne would take the cat and dog..."

"Oh, I forgot to tell you" - I interrupted. "Pam said she would be interested in leasing Redwing for a lesson horse if I go away."

"Oh, well - that's good. That's one animal taken care of. I'm sure she would be looked after properly under Pam's care. Are you okay with that?"

"Yeah, "I said. "It's much better for her to be used than to just waste away in the pasture all year. I thought Russell could keep her, but he wouldn't have a use for her. She can earn her keep at the stable."

Mom thought for a bit. Then she said, "I think I'll put an ad in the paper to rent the place. It might as well pay for itself rather than have it sit empty." I nodded my agreement. I didn't mention my idea of Russell living in it while we were gone. If we didn't get a renter in time, I would suggest that.

The next few weeks flew by in a blur. Russell and I buckled down and studied hard for our final exams. We both wanted to do well, and it seemed that when we were together we were either distracted by arguing about my leaving, or by being so attracted to each other, that we couldn't keep our hands off each other, and we ended up not getting much studying done. So we agreed to work alone.

Russell started a job with Buckerfields, the local feed company. He was working part-time until school was out and he still milked cows on the weekends, so he was kept busy. One of the perks of the job was that if there were any split or broken bags of feed, he could have them to take home. So we had a steady supply of chicken, horse, and dog food.

All too soon, exams were done, school was over, year-end parties were held, sad goodbyes were said, and my mom, Mrs. Donnelly and I were ready for our adventure overseas.

CHAPTER NINE

That last night before I was to fly to London, England, Russell picked me up in his truck and we drove around town, stopping for milkshakes at the Dairy Queen. Then we headed out on some country road. We were slurping the last of our chocolate and strawberry shakes when he drove under the Mission bridge and along a rough dirt road that went past a gravel pit that was a known party place. I hoped we weren't stopping there, and was relieved when he drove on past. The dirt road continued on a little ways and just kind of disappeared. There was a scraggly little beach on the right, and on the left, a tangle of blackberry vines and willow bushes grew with wild abandon. We hadn't said much to each other. We were both painfully aware that we had just hours left together. There was so much to be said, and so much left unsaid, that neither of us knew where to begin.

Russell stopped the truck, and slid out from behind the wheel towards me. He slumped against me with his face buried in my hair and neck. I could sense his misery and pain. I held him close and ran my fingers through his curly dark hair, and rubbed his shoulders and back.

He started kissing me on my neck, and at the same time he slipped his hand under my red cotton wrap-around skirt

64

and started up my leg. I don't know why I had worn a skirt that night; I hardly ever did. I think I just wanted to look pretty for him, but it was a mistake. His kisses were getting more and more insistent. I pushed on his chest and struggled to sit up. It was then I noticed that he had undone his fly and everything was hanging out. He took my hand and put it there and held it, pressing down. There was no mistaking what he wanted.

"No", I said. "Don't!" I tried to pull my hand away.

Russell said, "C'mon, let me give you something to remember me by."

"Russell, are you crazy?" I said. I was genuinely worried. I had never known him to be pushy like this. Instead of an answer, he started pulling at my underwear.

That was it! I was out of there! I felt behind me and grabbed the door handle. We both practically fell out of the truck when the door opened. I tried to slam it in his face but he was too quick. I started running, but he was right behind me and he grabbed my skirt and pulled. I felt the cotton rip as I was spun in a semi circle, and then I was sprawled on the rough gravelly sand. He was on top of me in an instant, and he was angry. He yanked the rest of my skirt off and tried to push into me.

I was sobbing and pounding on his shoulders with my fists. I could not push him off. He was too strong for me.

"Please Russell," I moaned, "Don't do this. I don't want it to be this way! No! Oh God...No!" He wasn't listening. In desperation I reached my arm out and felt around on the rough ground. My hand closed around a rock. I grabbed it and brought it down on the side of Russell's head. He let out a yell of pain and rolled away from me. I took the opportunity to kick him in the nuts. As he lay there moaning and cursing, I scrambled to my feet, grabbed my skirt, and ran for the truck. I jumped in and locked the doors. Then I sat there panting and crying, and berating myself for not ever having learned to drive a gearshift. I knew that even if I tried to turn the Ford around and get out of there, I would just stall it.

In about ten minutes Russell staggered over to the truck and tapped on the window, looking in at my tearstained face. "Let me in," he said. "I'll drive you home."

"Promise?" I asked.

He nodded.

I didn't really have a choice. It was too far to walk and I couldn't drive. I unlocked the doors.

He got in gingerly. I could tell he was sore, but I didn't give a rat's ass at that point. I was too mad for words. We drove home without a word being exchanged between us. I was waiting for an apology, but apparently, none was forthcoming.

In my driveway we sat apart with the motor running. He wouldn't look at me. "Russell," I said. "Let's not leave it like this. I know you're angry with me for leaving, but what you did tonight was despicable. If you had been sweet and gentle tonight, I probably *would* have made love with you. You know I want to. But I want it to be special. I want it to be romantic, and I want the timing to be just right. And now...I'm sorry, but we're out of time." I leaned over and kissed his cheek gently. "Goodbye."

He didn't answer, just kept starting straight ahead. I got out of the truck and went into the house. I heard the spray of gravel as he turned the truck around and sped out of the laneway.

CHAPTER TEN

I entered the darkened house, thankful that Mom had gone to bed. I went into the bathroom and washed my tear-stained face with cold water. My skirt had a big rip in it, and my white blouse was filthy. My hair was a mess; my eyes were swollen and my bare arms were scratched and dirty. Looking at the apparition in the mirror, I started to shake. I ran the hot water into the tub, shed my dirt-stained clothes, and sank gratefully into the soothing water. Ying-Yang clawed at the door, wanting in. I opened the door a crack, and she sauntered in and hopped up on the ledge of the tub, where she liked to sit while I had a bath. The scenario of my near rape played over and over in my mind. Many emotions washed over me, along with the hot water. I felt very confused, angry, and sad that things had turned out this way.

Resolving to burn my skirt and top in the burning barrel in the morning, I eased out of the tub, dried off and crawled into bed. Ying-Yang snuggled up under the covers with me, and as I stroked her head and back I said to her, " Why are animals so easy to get along with compared to humans?" She just licked my hand with her raspy tongue, and purred in contentment.

I didn't think I had slept at all, but before I knew it I smelled coffee and heard Mom moving around in the kitchen. We had a lot to do to get ready to leave today. The beds had to be stripped and the laundry all done. All our personal things that we weren't taking on the trip had been packed away and put in boxes in the basement. Mom had put ads in the paper, and notices up around town, and had got a call from the local R.C.M.P. detachment. A young officer and his family had just been transferred to Abbotsford and needed a place to rent. Mike, Debbie and their two little girls came out to see the place and they just loved it. They had good references, and they signed a lease for a year. Perfect! They wanted to get some goats and sheep and they asked us if that would be okay. We didn't mind that. Redwing was already at the stable, under Pam's care, so we had that big barn with nothing in it but the bantams. The family also agreed to care for Buckwheat and Ying-Yang. They wanted to get their own pets eventually, but they were happy to look after ours in the meantime. Mom made some agreement with Russell's dad to look after the place if anything needed doing, and to collect the rent. He was also going to bring food for the cat and dog from the broken bags that Russell brought home from Buckerfields. It was terribly hard to leave our precious pets in the care of strangers, but at least they could stay in their own home and we knew these people would be good to them.

After breakfast, Mom was doing the dishes and I was cleaning my room when Russell's mom phoned. I listened in on the conversation, but it seemed pretty normal; they were just saying their goodbyes. Then she asked to speak to me. I called out to Mom, "Please tell her I'll call her right back. I'm busy with something for a few minutes." Mom had asked how it went with Russell last night, and I couldn't bring myself to tell her what happened. I just said that he was pretty upset, but he'd get over it.

When Mom went down to the basement to fold the bedding, I grabbed the phone and called Russell's number. Marcie answered. We made small talk for a minute or two, while she wished me all the best in my horse course. Then she asked, "Is Russell with you?" I could detect the worry in her voice.

"Uh...no," I said, "He brought me home before midnight last night. Isn't he home?" *Oh- oh*, I thought, *What's he done now?*

"No," Marcie said. "He didn't come home last night, and I thought maybe he was over there. He was supposed to milk cows this morning, but he didn't show up, so Ben went out to do it."

"Well, that's strange," I said. "Maybe he took Sunny and went up on the mountain. He *was* kind of upset."

Marcie said, "No, his truck's not here, and Sunny is in the corral. Do you have any idea where he might be?"

I felt sick inside. *What should I tell her? That her son was a rapist?* I decided to tell her the truth.

"Um...Marcie," I began. "I don't know where Russell is, but you should know that things got pretty ugly with us last night."

"What do you mean, ugly?" she asked, concern rising in her voice.

"Well..." I choked back tears. "Russell got rough with me, and tried to force me to have sex with him, and I..."

"Oh, Lindsey, I am so sorry!" she interrupted. "Are you all right?"

"Yeah...I'm okay...just shaken up. But I had to hit him over the head with a rock, and I kicked him where it hurts too."

"Good for you!" Marcie said. "It's good you're going away and breaking up for a while. Russell's got some growing up to do."

"Yes, he does." I agreed. "But I'm sorry it came to this, and I hope he's all right. I do love him, you know."

"Yes, I know Lindsey. You're doing the right thing."

I managed to blurt out, "I feel terrible leaving the country, not even knowing if he's home safe. I doubt if he'll call me, but would you let me know when he gets home? We'll be leaving here around noon for my sister's, and they're taking us to the airport at four o'clock." I gave Marcie Maryanne's number, and she promised to get in touch with me before I left.

As I worked through the rest of the cleaning and packing, my mind was in turmoil. *Where was Russell? Was he all right? Had he had an accident?* I prayed for the phone to ring before we had to leave. It didn't.

Just before noon, the Robson family arrived with their possessions. It felt weird seeing them take their things into our house and start to make it their home. The two girls made at least five trips down to the barn to see the chickens, and when we finally drove away, they were playing ball with Buckwheat on the lawn. He loved kids and would be happy with them, but I couldn't help but wonder how he and Ying Yang would feel when we didn't come back. I would miss them both.

Mrs. Donnelly was ready, and had a whole contingent of nurses and fellow residents gathered around to see us off. Our poor little car was loaded to the gunnels with the luggage for all three of

us. We drove past the Eagle Ridge
Equestrian Center and I craned my neck
for a glimpse of Redwing in the outdoor
pens, but I didn't see her. Mom turned
the car onto the freeway and headed
towards the city.

The rest of the afternoon was a
blur of activity; getting to the airport,
going through customs, getting our
entire luggage checked through, saying
tearful goodbyes to the family, and then
the three of us, Mrs. Donnelly in her
wheelchair, waving a last farewell before
we went through the gate to board the
big 707. I had not heard from Marcie, and
I agonized over Russell's whereabouts.
There was nothing I could do, but worry.

Soon after takeoff, a meal was
served, and then darkness descended and
I fell into a restless sleep. We were
actually somewhere between Winnipeg
and northern Ontario, when Russell
finally came home; too late for Marcie to
let me know that he was safe.

I didn't find out for almost a full
year where Russell had been the previous
night. Not until I returned home the
following fall and we got back together,
did I hear the details of that night.

He was angry and he just drove
until some of that anger wore off. Then
the remorse set in. He felt so badly for
what he had done - or almost done. He
considered killing himself for a while, but

73

then thought it would be too much of a shock for his parents and they didn't deserve that. He stopped at a bar, and purchased a large bottle of coke, and a bottle of rum. He poured out half of the coke and topped it up with alcohol. Then he drove out on the back roads for a couple of hours, drinking and feeling sorry for himself. Finally he just passed out at the wheel. The truck stalled and rolled into the ditch. Luckily for him, the ditches on the Sumas Prairie are shallow, and he didn't get hurt. He slept until late in the morning and woke with a terrible headache. He stumbled out of the truck and peed in the ditch and then promptly threw up. It was starting to get hot. He laid down in the shade of the truck and slept again, until late afternoon.

When he arrived home, expecting to catch hell, Marcie hugged him with tears in her eyes. She whispered in his ear, "Lindsey told me what happened, and it's all right. She's gone, but she still loves you. You've got some fences to mend."

When we arrived at Heathrow Airport early the next morning, I just had to call the Livingston's to see if Russell was home. Thank God, he was. I could now relax and enjoy the trip, knowing he was all right.

CHAPTER ELEVEN

Mrs. Donnelly insisted we call her Victoria. She was a lively and talkative character. She had traveled extensively, and was well-educated, well read, and had opinions on everything. Her soft, curly hair, which was completely white, framed her lively face. Her eyes were a violet blue color, and her complexion was still lovely, even at the age of seventy. She had some difficulty walking, so had to be in a wheelchair for sightseeing or going out to dinner. She needed minimal help for bathing and getting into bed, so she really wasn't that hard to look after.

She was generous with her money. She liked wine with dinner, and she encouraged us to order whatever we wanted from the hotel menus. She would laugh gaily, saying, "We might as well enjoy life. Come on, let's have dessert!" She and Mom seemed to get along famously. I hoped that the good spirits would last for the duration of the trip.

We spent a couple of days in London, and did all the touristy things like visiting Buckingham Palace to see the Changing of the Guards, going to St. Paul's Cathedral, Madam Tussauds Wax Museum, and the Tower of London. Then we boarded a train at Euston Station for Scotland.

Victoria had cousins in Glasgow and that was our first stop. I was so impressed with the beauty of the English and Scottish countryside. I was quite taken with the Tudor and thatched cottages, the profusion of hedges and flowering shrubs; the windy little country roads on which we frequently saw shepherds herding their woolly sheep. I was almost sorry when the train entered the busy train yard at our destination.

The McNeil's, a rosy and rotund little couple, met us. Dora and Scotty made us welcome in their modest home. I was amazed at how much these people ate. They liked their afternoon tea complete with sandwiches and cakes as well as three main meals a day. After a day visiting with them, we all piled into the car and Scotty drove us to our next destination – Oban, by the sea.

I loved Oban. We said our goodbyes to the McNeil's and checked into the Corran Hotel, right on the esplanade. I couldn't wait to get out and walk along the beach. The wind was a little blustery, which made the waves pound madly on the shoreline. Gulls wheeled and dipped and called, checking the seaweed along the shore for anything to eat. Mom pushed Victoria in her wheelchair along the seawall, and we met after our walk at McTavish's Kitchen where the choices on the menu were Fish and Chips or Steak and Kidney Pie. That's all. Oh, not quite. For dessert, there was a choice of Pear Belle Helene, or ice cream.

In the evening, we went down to the lounge at the Corran. There was plenty of that good old Scottish whisky flowing, along with copious amounts of beer. At the mike in the corner, a young fellow with a flaming red beard was playing the guitar and singing Irish and Scottish folksongs. He noticed me right away. I saw him looking my way a couple of times between songs, and when he got a break, he came over to our table.

"Haloo, there," he greeted us in his thick highland brogue. "I spied the wee lassie here singing along with all me songs. I'm Stuart McKenzie".

His voice had such a wonderful lilt to it. We found ourselves picking up on it and doing the same. Introductions were made all around. Stuart brought his beer over and joined us and proceeded to question us thoroughly about Canada. Then he asked me, "Will ye come up and sing a wee song wi' me, lass? Do ye ken the 'Bonny Bonny Banks of Loch Lomand?'" I said that I knew that one, so Stuart grabbed me by the hand and pulled me up to the mike. The Shandy I had just drunk must have given me some courage. Mom and Victoria were smiling their encouragement as well, as Stuart and I sang in harmony the beautiful old

77

tune. We got a great round of applause, and Stuart launched into Robbie Burns' 'Will Ye No Come Back Again?' I ended up doing a whole set with Stuart. It was great fun. The songs I didn't know, I just harmonized or hummed along with. Nobody minded – they were all half cut and having a great time. People started buying me drinks and yelling "Hello Canada!"
I had the sense to know I couldn't possibly keep up with these drinkers. I sipped on a beer just because the singing made me dry, but I ignored the glasses that were set before me. After a while I noticed that Mom and Victoria were gone. I had a great time singing, laughing and visiting with the folk of Oban before going "awa to my bed" at two a.m. Stuart gave me a big hug and a kiss on the cheek, saying " I've had a great time wi' ye lass. You're vera bonnie!" I think he was disappointed that we were leaving the next day for Edinburgh.

At Edinburgh, Victoria wanted to visit two sisters that she had gone to school with. Kate and Chrissie lived together in a small stone cottage. They didn't have room for Mom and me, so we left Victoria there and stayed at a lovely little bed and breakfast near the castle. We had a tour of the Edinburgh Castle the next day and

then we picked Victoria up and boarded
the train for the Highlands of Scotland.
"How was your visit with the
sisters?" Mom asked.
Victoria replied, "Och, they're so
frugal! Their house is cold and they're too
stingy to turn up the heat. For breakfast
they *share* an egg! Can you believe it?
Two grown women behaving like they're
paupers. They've both been teachers and
never married, so I'm sure they have
money. It's so foolish not to spend it!"
Mom and I were grateful that Mrs.
Donnelly didn't mind spending hers.

For the next two weeks, we visited
Victoria's relatives and friends at
Stornaway, on the Isle of Lewis, Portree,
on the Isle of Skye, and even stayed in a
castle on the Isle of Barra in the Outer
Hebrides.
At Stornaway, I walked down to the
wharves to watch the fishermen bringing
in the day's catch. I was taken by
surprise when a young man in rubber
boots and raincoat stepped off his boat
and kissed me. He and his mates had
seen me watching, and he did it on a
dare. They had a great laugh, and I didn't
really mind. When they were finished
unloading, they came and talked to me,
curious as to where I had come from. The
young man gave me some of their fish to
take home. They were called 'Kippers'

and they were very good fried up for breakfast. There were hardly any trees on the Isle of Lewis. Those that survived the severe weather were twisted and gnarled, like old men bent before the wind. The place had a wild beauty about it.

Skye did too, with its beautiful blue craggy peaks and heather covered moors. The stormy ocean beat a steady tattoo on the ancient rocks. I loved to walk the beaches and trails with visions of Bonnie Prince Charlie, Dame Flora MacDonald, or Sir Donald Urquhart, my ancient ancestors with me in spirit.

On Barra, slashing rain and wild winds confined us to the castle in the bay. The power went out and even the generator wouldn't run. The few guests gathered in the great room where a peat fire gave off a rosy glow but little heat. The proprietor brought out the whisky and proceeded to get very drunk. He burst into song and regaled us with tales of the Scottish highlands. Wrapped in blankets, sipping the golden drink by the fire while the candles sputtered and flared and the Bard of Barra entertained us was a memory I'll not soon forget.

Back in London at the end of August, Mom and Victoria prepared for their cruise down the coast of France and Spain. I assisted with their luggage and went on board the ship with them at

Southampton. Before it sailed, Mom gave me a paper with Dad's address and phone number on it. I had wondered about him many times since we were in England. I asked Mom, "Don't you want to see him?"

"No", she smiled wistfully. "He belongs in a past life. He's not connected to me anymore, but he'll always be a part of you. I think you should contact him. He may be someone to turn to here if things get rough."

She hugged me long and hard, hating to let go of her youngest. I had never been on my own and I knew it was very hard for her to leave me in a strange country. I hugged Victoria too, and thanked her for the wonderful trip. She wished me all the best. With promises to write each other with tales of our adventures, we reluctantly parted.

The decks were thronged with people throwing gaily-colored streamers and balloons over the sides as the Carinthia eased away from the docks. With the horns blowing and billows of steam gushing from the great funnels, the huge white ship turned ponderously and sailed out of the harbor. Tears streamed down my face, as the figures of Mom and Victoria, waving bravely, got smaller, smaller, and then disappeared. I knew they would be crying too.

I had never felt so all-alone. It was a strange, yet somewhat exhilarating feeling being on my own in a huge city, not knowing a single soul. I had wanted to stay at a Youth Hostel so that I might meet other young people who were traveling, but Victoria had paid for my room at the hotel for the next few days, so it would have been foolish not to have taken advantage of her kindness.

I soon got used to my own company. Several times I tried to get up the courage to call my dad, but I couldn't do it. He was a stranger to me, and I was still trying to sort out my feelings for him. I resented the fact that he left our family for another life so far away.

I was due at the Fulmer School of Equitation in four days time. I had talked to Ms. Bryant on the phone and arranged for her to meet me at the train station on the 7th of September. In the meantime, I had fun exploring London. I found it fascinating to wander through the markets of Petticoat Lane. I went to the British Museum and met interesting people from all over the world at Piccadilly Square. I took the underground railway known as the tube to various parts of the city. Then I would come up and walk the streets – sometimes it would be rows and rows of look-alike tenement houses, another time it would be cottages, or mansions of the gentry. I found all of it interesting. I walked the trails on Hampstead Heath and skirted warily around drug addicts, pimps and prostitutes in Soho Square. I was careful not go out after dark. I had my evening meal in the hotel, and after a day of sightseeing and walking, I was content to stay in my room just reading or watching T.V.

On the 7th, I took a taxi to the train station and headed out to the beautiful Somerset countryside.

CHAPTER TWELVE

On the train, I happened to meet another girl that was going to Fulmer. I had noticed her paddock boots and riding helmet tied on to the outside of her backpack. We started out with shy smiles at each other, recognizing a common bond of traveling alone, being close in age, and maybe having a horsy connection too.

Screwing up my courage, I moved into an empty seat beside her and introduced myself.

"Hi, Lindsey," she said, shaking my hand. "It's great to meet you."
Her accent sounded strange to my ears. It was somewhat like the English, but different again. "I'm Joan Hall, from Port Elizabeth, right at the tip of South Africa," she told me. I liked Joan right away. Her dark brown eyes sparkled with her smile, which showed even, white teeth. Her short dark curly hair reminded me of Russell's. I wondered, fleetingly, what he was doing, and if he was still angry. I had written to him, telling him all about our tour of Scotland, but somehow, I didn't expect a reply.

Joan was saying, "We should all be on this train. There are four international students coming to work at Fulmer this year. They alternate between British and overseas students." I was going to ask how she knew this, when she suggested, "Let's walk through the cars, and try to find the others."

""Okay," I agreed. Then she answered my unspoken question. "My dad asked who the other students were, and was told that there was one from Canada - that's you - one from New Zealand, one from Sweden, and myself. So we've just got to find ourselves a Swede and a Kiwi."

"Oh well," I laughed, "that shouldn't be too hard. Let's go."

Finding the Swede was easy. In the next car, we both spied a young girl with long blonde braids and blue eyes. "That's her," Joan whispered. "Hey, are you related? You look quite a bit alike."

"Yeah," I joked. "Our father was a well-traveled Viking."

Joan grinned, and said to the girl. "Are you a Fulmer student?"

"Ya," she nodded, "And you are the others?" Her accent was like a melody, each vowel rising and falling like musical notes. We introduced ourselves and then she came with us, lurching down the aisles of the moving train to find the last member of our team.

Our little troupe eventually found Donalda Smythe from Christchurch, N.Z. She was a quiet girl with a square face, gray eyes and mousy brown shoulder-length hair. "'allo mites," she smiled.

"Mites," I said, "Aren't they tiny bugs?" They all laughed.

"You've got an accent too, you know," Donalda said to me. A Canadian one. Mites, mates, it's all the same." I thought about this. I didn't realize that I had an accent too.

All four of us made our way down the narrow aisles of the train, back to our car where we proceeded to get to know each other, as four women together will do.

We entered the pretty little village of Taunton early in the afternoon. When we exited the train, and stood in a knot on the platform, a solid looking, no nonsense kind of woman approached us.

"Well then," she said, "You've found one another it would seem. I'm Liz Bryant. How do you do?" She proceeded to shake each one of us by the hand. Introductions were made all around and then Liz led us to the 'lorry', a two-seater truck. We threw our gear into the back of it, and piled in. It still seemed odd to me to have the driver steering the vehicle on the right side and also to be driving on the left, totally opposite to what I was used to.

I studied Liz as we drove and talked. Her graying hair was pulled back into a ponytail that she had stuck through the back opening of a baseball cap. Her skin was browned and wrinkled, weather-beaten, I guessed from a life lived outdoors in wind and rain. She seemed robust, strong and healthy, and I had a premonition that we would have to work very hard to keep up to her.

"Well, here we are," she said, as we drove between two low, curving brick walls on either side of the narrow road. On the right above a profusion of flowering shrubs, was a sign that stated "Fulmer School of Equitation". There was a woodcut of a jumping horse and rider on it.

Liz drove slowly up the lane past sheds with paddocks full of horses, past a small red barn, and a much larger stone barn. We passed a small cottage that she informed us was her's and her 'man's'.

"Who's your man then?" asked Joan. Trust her to ask; she was the bold one. "Oh, Joe's me man," Liz smiled. "He's a great cook, and I'm useless in the kitchen. He's the chief gardener around here, and also Mr. Fixit. If anything's broken, Joe can fix it."

Then she added, "I'll take you girls on up to the house where you'll be staying and get you settled in. Then we'll have tea and I'll show you the stables. You'll be feeding the horses tonight and then we'll get you your work schedules for the morning.

The house where we girls were quartered in a huge upstairs room was called Bredalbane House. Liz told me right off that the accent was on the 'dal', not the 'bred'. The house was very old, and a bit shabby looking, but had been very grand in its day. It was three stories high, a real English Tudor mansion with yellow/brown stone between solid dark, oak trim. On the main floor there was a sitting room with fireplace, T.V. coffee tables, shelves with books and puzzles, and a writing table. I wondered about the work schedule Liz had mentioned, and if there would be any free time to lounge around in this room. Across the hallway, was the dining room, set up with a long table, already set for the evening meal. The kitchen was behind that with its huge gas stove, big butcher-block counters, and countless cupboards and shelves. There was a small table, but it looked like all the taking of meals was in the dining room. Another smaller room off the dining room was an office and across from that there was another large room that had been made into a classroom.

"Here is where you do your book learning." Liz told us. "We get different instructors in to teach you about the business end of running a large stable."

Back in the hallway, a wide stairway led to the upstairs. We were shown to a huge room that contained four single

beds, one in each corner of the room.
Beside each bed there was a dresser and
end table. The distance between each set-
up gave a semblance of privacy, yet we
were all together for company. I liked the
looks of it, and said so.

Liz said, "You can move the beds
around any way you want – even put them
together." She shrugged, "It's been done
before." Then she showed us 'the loo'
which was also large and was next door
to our room. There was a huge claw-
footed tub, separate shower, washbasin,
shelves for towels and personal items,
and of course a toilet. I wondered if one
'loo' would be enough for four girls that
had to go at the same time. Liz seemed
to read my thoughts for next she showed
us another little bathroom, next to the
big one that contained a toilet and
washbasin only.

Donalda asked quietly, "Doesn't
anyone else live here except us?"

"Oh yes," Liz told us. Mrs. Culvers,
the cook, has her bedroom just down the
hall there, and Jeremy, the kitchen boy
sleeps downstairs. They've just gone out
to the market."

"Who owns this place?" Britt-Marie asked,
her big blue eyes wide and questioning.

Liz answered with a smile, "The
owners are very wealthy, and live on the
Italian Riviera. This place is just a tax
write-off for them. They do come to visit

once in a while, bringing their staff with them. At such times, they open the suite on the top floor and stay there. So...there are only the ghosts up there for now..."

"Ghosts?" we all chorused at once. Liz chuckled. "Just kidding." Then, seeing the worried looks on our faces, she added, "Come on, let's go down and make some tea."

CHAPTER THIRTEEN

After 'tea', which consisted of a pot of tea, scones and cheese, we went down to the barn. We were informed that the pantry in the kitchen would be locked after the supper dishes were done, but we could make tea, coffee, or hot chocolate. Liz advised us to buy our own biscuits or bread if we wanted snacks in the evenings, as none were provided.

The U-shaped shed row faced on to a cobblestone courtyard. There were six stalls on each side and twelve on the long side. Behind each stall was an adjoining paddock for two horses. A smaller building facing the courtyard housed the hay, grain, and straw. The large covered riding arena was situated behind the long row of stalls and paddocks. Across the laneway, in front of the house, there was a smaller outdoor ring. Behind this there were more pastures and paddocks with shelters for the yearlings, and up a winding road past several cottages the brood mares and stallions were kept. We would see them tomorrow – right now, Liz put us to work doing evening rounds.

She said, "You'll each have six horses to look after. They've been chosen for you on the basis of your experience and what you told us in your applications. You'll each have two young ones to break in, and four you'll be taking your lessons on, training for clients, and preparing for shows."

Liz beckoned us to follow, and obediently, we did. She opened a door. "Here is the tack room." We all peeked in to see rows of gleaming English saddles and bridles all neatly arranged on racks and hooks. The smell of glycerin saddle soap assailed our senses. I could see we'd be spending some time keeping the tack spotless.

Back outside, Liz pointed to the tools hanging outside of the stalls. She said, "There are four sets of tools – broom, rake, fork, shovel, and wheelbarrow. They are to be hung up on the appropriate hooks when not in use." She wasn't asking politely, it was an order. We all nodded dutifully. Liz continued, "You'll notice also each horse's halter is hanging beside the stall door." She stopped, crossed her arms, and looked at us in turn. "Now, listen carefully. I'm only going to tell you this once." We paid attention.

"You will muck out the stalls in the morning and leave them bare to dry while the horses are turned out. They go out rain or shine, but they are blanketed if it is cold and wet. There's a bit of an overhang they can stand under if it's very rainy. Now, while they're out, you take your barrow over to the shed and get two bales of straw. If you're strong enough and can balance it, you can bring three. You use half a bale for each stall. The floors are clay, so we don't have to bed too deeply for the riding horses. The foaling stalls are bedded deeper, but we don't have to concern ourselves with that until spring." Liz paused and ran a hand through her graying hair. She said, "Fill up the water buckets which you will have scrubbed in the morning. Then go to the feed room and mix up your horse's ration – I'll show you that in a minute – and put his feed in his box. Use your barrow again to bring the hay over. One bale will generally feed four animals, so you'll need six bales altogether."

I was getting anxious to see the horses, but Liz said, "Right! Now, you have to match up the right feed ration with the right horses, so now we'll go over to the feed room."

"Why don't they all get the same?" asked Britt Marie, as we all trooped into the shed.

"Can any of you answer that?" asked Liz as she cast her eyes over the group.

"Well", I ventured, I would guess that the young horses get more grain than the mature ones, just because they are still growing...and possibly one that is working hard will get more than one that is idle."

"That's correct," our teacher said. "It also depends on their weight and temperament. For instance, One of Lindsey's is a pony and he doesn't need any grain – he only gets a handful because he knows the others get grain, and we don't want him to be a sourpuss."

Joan laughed. "I had a pony like that at home. We called him Mr. Piggy."

Inside, the scrubbed feed pails were lined up in four rows of six. Each one had a number painted on it. Everything had a prescribed order here. I made a mental note not to screw up the system.

Liz handed each one of us a card on which was written our horses names, stall numbers, and feeding information. I had the stalls numbered seven to twelve, one half of the long shed row. I looked at the horses' names with interest. I would meet them in person soon.

#7 – Montgomery: Dark bay gelding. Dales Pony, 2 yrs.

#8 – Desert Fire – Gray Thoroughbred gelding. 2 yrs.

#9 – Chester – Chestnut. Irish Cob gelding. 7 yrs.

#10 – Blackjack – Black Thoroughbred gelding. 4 yrs.

#11 – Mustard Sauce – Chestnut Thor.cross mare. 6 yrs.

#12 – Tinkerbelle – Bay Anglo-Arab mare.12 yrs.

Later on in the classroom we would learn how to balance rations with the proper proportions of protein to carbohydrates, but for now we just put the prescribed number of scoops of oats, bran, or corn into each bucket. Liz left us on our own to prepare the stalls and bring in our horses.

When we finished our chores and went up to Bredalbane House for supper of beef stew and biscuits, Liz gave each of us a timetable. Whoever coined the phrase "Working Pupil" was right on the mark. Liz grinned, anticipating the groans that followed when she announced: "The horses eat first, ladies. They'll be expecting their breakfast at 0700 hours. Don't be late! Feed your stalled horses first. Then, Britt-Marie and Donalda will go up with me to feed the broodmares and studs."

Joan put her hand up to ask a question. "How many are there?"

"We have two stallions and a band of twenty-three mares." She looked at Joan and I. "You two will go and check the yearling colts and fillies. Joe will show you how to feed them. Tomorrow, we'll switch. When you are finished, come up for breakfast at eight o'clock. Then at eight-thirty you'll go down and muck the stalls, and you'll each do a training session with your young horses. I'll be supervising that, and next week we have a riding instructor coming to teach dressage and jumping. Mark McTaggart is a graduate of the Weedon School of Equitation, which is quite famous, and he has been a member of the Taunton Hunt for four seasons. He's done Pony Club, and ridden in the military, so he comes very well qualified."

Trust Joan to ask "Is he married?"

There was laughter all around, but genuine interest too. Liz gave us a stern look. "Now girls... Mark is quite a dashing young fellow, but he considers himself quite a dandy. I'm warning you now, to be careful. Don't get involved with any of the staff." She paused a moment, letting this sink in. Then she continued, "Dinner is from twelve to one, and then in the afternoon, we'll be doing lessons and training on your finished horses, and office work. Tea is at four o'clock, and as you know, evening chores from four-thirty to six. Your evenings are free, but you will have studying to do, and in foaling season we do a rotation of foal-watch duty. You'll each have a different day and a half off each week; on those days, the rest of you will pick up the care and feeding of the extra horses. Any questions?"

There were none. I think we were all wondering if there were enough hours in the day, and enough energy to accomplish all the tasks that had to be done each day. I was already dropping with exhaustion, and desperately needing sleep.

CHAPTER FOURTEEN

There was no dawn on our first day at
Fulmer. It was dark and rainy at six-thirty
in the morning. It felt like the middle of
the night when Joan shook me awake. I
wasn't a morning person. I found it hard
to get going early, and almost impossible
to work without fuel in my tank – at least
a cup of coffee for a kick-start. I
protested inwardly, but already was
forcing myself to adopt that stiff upper
lip that was so famous in Britain.

There was not much talk as we
dressed in barn clothes, donned our
raincoats and wellies (rubber boots) and
made our way down to the stables.

I soon forgot my hunger as we were
met with joyous whinnies of welcome
from all the horses. Twenty-four pairs of
luminous brown eyes watched our every
move as we started to bring the feed
over, and there was excited head tossing,
snorting, pawing and banging of feed
buckets as the horses anticipated their
morning feed.

"Good morning Monty," I greeted
my shaggy Dales pony. He snatched
greedily at the hay in my arms. I pushed
him away, and gave his neck a scratch as
I put his hay into the manger. "You're a
very rude fellow," I told him. "We'll have
to work on that."

"Hello, beautiful boy, " I said to Desert Fire as the gray greeted me at the stall door with an inquisitive whoosh in my face. Next door, Chester banged on his stall door. Although the chubby chestnut had a plain face, it was full of character. His jagged white blaze, pendulous lower lip, and long ears gave him a comical appearance. "All right, you clown," I said to him. "Get back, here's your breakfast."

At Blackjack's stall I got a different reception. He met me with ears back and a sour expression on his face. "Easy boy," I soothed. Last night when I went to bring him in, he had charged past me into the stall without letting me catch him. *This one would be a challenge.*I thought. I eased out of the stall as he gave the wall behind him a resounding smack with a hind hoof. *Ooh, temperamental!*

The mares were sweet, polite and had nice stall manners, keeping a respectful distance while I fed them. Of the two, I immediately favored Tinkerbelle over Mustard Sauce. Her Arab breeding showed in her large lively eyes and pointy ears. She looked intelligent and kind. Mustard Sauce was kind of a plain horse. She looked to be solid and honest, but with not much personality.

As the days sped by, we girls settled into the routine of mucking stalls, feeding, grooming, polishing tack, starting our young horses on the lunge line, and riding our lesson horses. It seemed we were forever picking up manure. If the horses dropped their buns on the cobbled courtyard, or in the shed row where they were cross-tied and groomed before saddling, we had to clean it up right away. We also had to pick up the manure in their paddocks where they were turned out each day, and after our lessons we had to leave the arena clean. Mom's words came back to be many times, *"You don't want to be mucking stalls forever, do you?"*

I thought of Mom and Victoria frequently as I worked. I tried to imagine what they were doing on board the luxurious liner. As I sloshed through the rain and mud, I pictured the sunshine and warmth as Mom pushed Victoria in her wheelchair along the promenade deck, somewhere down the coast of Spain. As we ate our breakfast porridge, I thought of the plates of tropical fruit, cold meats and fluffy omelets that would be served in the opulent dining room. Later on they would dine on fresh seafood and have their choice of decadent desserts. Up at the house, we could probably look forward to Shepherds Pie and a pudding.

Our meals were okay – God knows we were hungry enough to eat anything when we came in from the barn chores - it's just that Mrs. Culvers didn't have much of an imagination in the kitchen, and soon her limited repertoire began to repeat itself.

I was happy for Mom that she was getting this chance of a lifetime to travel and to experience the cuisine of other countries. For myself...well...I had made my choice, and I did not regret it. I was learning so much, not only about the horse business, but also about myself. When I was so cold or exhausted that I felt I couldn't lift a finger, I would somehow find some inner strength to go on and finish the job. Instead of dissolving into tears I would grit my teeth and try harder. Just being around the horses always lifted my spirits. They were the true teachers, not the human ones.

Mark McTaggart caused quite a stir when he arrived one afternoon at teatime in his bright red Porsche sports car.

"Hello love!" he shouted, as he leapt from the car and enfolded Liz in his arms. They obviously knew each other from the horseshow circuit or something. At any rate, Joe just stood there and grinned, not seeming to mind. Mark released Liz and grabbed Joe's hand in a hearty shake. "Hello, you old bastard!" he said, nearly shaking Joe off his feet. Then he turned to us girls who were standing there gawking, somewhat shocked at what he had called Joe.

Already, some exchanged glances between us had confirmed that we all thought Mark was pretty darn attractive. He was tall – over six feet, broad shouldered but slim from the waist down. His short-sleeved polo shirt and riding breeches showed off his muscular physique.

Britt-Marie nudged me and whispered, "How old do you think he is?"

Donalda, whom we now had nicknamed Kiwi, or sometimes Donnie, whispered back, "Too old for you girl."

Joan giggled, "I think he's cute! Look at those sparkly blue eyes." When Mark turned his attention to us, those sparkly blue eyes looked directly into ours as Liz introduced each one of us. His wide smile, open inquisitive expression and his Irish brogue all added to his charm.

We all had sort of a crush on him, and tried our best to please him in our riding lessons. He was a tough taskmaster. In jumping lessons he would shout at me, "Come on Canada! Get your bottom up out of that saddle or I'll have to give it a whack with my crop!" He'd grin and strut around looking important and slap the whip against his riding boots. I would cringe with embarrassment at the thought of him spanking me, but I'd sure get up higher on my horse's withers next time I approached a jump. He almost never gave us a compliment, and we never felt we were progressing much.

CHAPTER FIFTEEN

I was making some progress with the cranky black gelding, Blackjack. That first week, while the other girls were watching TV, reading, or having a bath after supper, I would go down to the stable and just sit with Blackjack. At first he resented me being there, and in truth I was somewhat afraid to be near him. I got a mounting block, put it just inside the stall door, and moving slowly, slid in and sat down.

"Hi Blackjack," I said. "Why are you so darn crabby?" I had an apple in my pocket, and I took it out and took a bite. His ears pricked forward and then flattened and he waved his head menacingly.

"Oh, don't be such a darn fool," I told him. "I think you're just bluffing." He kicked the wall. "Has somebody hurt you?" I talked softly, munching on the apple. I could tell he was interested in it, but he wasn't going to give in. "You're not mean, are you?" I asked him. "I think you're just scared." I held out the apple and he looked at it longingly, but he wouldn't come towards me to get it.

Finally, after about a week of these nightly visits and chats, I could see Blackjack start to relax and even look forward to my presence. The first night that he took the piece of apple out of my hand, he reached out his neck as far as he could without taking a step towards me. Then he grabbed it and threw his head up as he backed up. "Hey, boy," I soothed. I'm not going to hit you. Somebody has beaten you, haven't they? Why would anyone want to be mean to you? You're so beautiful, and smart."

After that, he got braver and began to trust me. As long as I stayed still he would come up to take the apple treat out of my hand. I learned not to make any sudden moves around him, especially if I had a broom or fork in my hands. He would immediately be on the defensive and would bite or kick. I rode him a few times in lessons, but he was hard to handle, spooky and fractious. Once when one of the barn cats jumped down from a railing, he spun and bolted, very nearly unseating me. I spent the whole lesson just circling the spot where he had bolted, but he wouldn't go near it. Mark wanted me to use the whip on him, and force him to obey, but I didn't want to ruin the trust we were building, and I refused to hit him. Mark just shrugged his shoulders and walked away. I knew he was angry with me, but at that moment, I didn't care.

I caught up with Liz in the office one afternoon and asked about the black gelding's background. She told me, "I didn't really know much about him when we agreed to take him for training. We were told he'd been backed and ridden and that he just needed steady work. Since you re-trained your racehorse yourself, we thought we'd give you a chance to see what you could do with the rascal. If you don't think you can handle him, don't be ashamed to give it up. We'll tell the owners that he's an outlaw, and we'll just ship him. I 'm sure it won't be a surprise to them. I don't want you to get hurt."

"I'm being very careful around him, Liz," I said. I'm sure he's been beaten. He's harboring some awful resentment. I'd like to keep on trying. I think I'm starting to gain his trust now."

Liz rested her chin on her hands. "As long as you or the horse doesn't get hurt. We'll give it till Christmas and if he hasn't come around by then, I think he'll have to go."

"Fair enough." I grinned.

I was getting to be Blackjack's pal in the stall. My next challenge was to catch him out in his paddock. He always gave me the run around and then charged past me into his stall. I decided to teach him to come to me. One night at evening chores, I brought all the other horses in first, leaving him out alone. This he hated, and he ran around greatly agitated, whinnying his head off. I left his stall door closed and walked out to him. He charged, thinking he would run right into his stall. I threw the halter and lead at his face as he approached and held up my hands to slow him down. He swerved around me and ran to the corner, shaking his head. I approached him again. Same thing. He got the halter in his face, and he didn't get to go in. He stopped and turned to look at me. I dropped my hands and relaxed my body. "Good boy," I said. I walked toward him, but he turned his butt to me and looked over his shoulder in a threatening manner. Immediately, I chased him with the halter and rope. "Git!" I shouted. "If you're going to be nasty, you can do a few laps around your pen!" I chased him around until I saw his ear flick towards me. I stopped and stood still again. He stopped too and looked at me. "Good boy," I said, and held out the apple. He took a step toward me, wanting the apple, but he wouldn't look at me. His eyes were on the stall door. I jumped in the air and waved the halter at him. "Git!" I yelled again. Surprised, he tore off in a circle around me; head high, eyes bugged, tail over his back. This time when he stopped, he turned his body toward me and waited. I walked up to him and rubbed his shoulder. "Good boy, good fella," I said soothingly. "That's right. You're figuring it out. Good for you." Then I walked away and stood with my back to him. Blackjack looked at the closed door of his stall. Then he looked at me. He lowered his head, and snorting softly through his nostrils, he came and stood behind me. I turned and offered him the apple, which he took politely from my hand. Then I held up the halter and he stood quietly while I slipped it on his head and did up the throatlatch. A round of quiet applause burst from the paddock fence. It was now dark, and I had not seen the group gather to watch my performance.

"Well done!" called Joan, and the rest of the group echoed her compliments. Even Mark was there, and he said, "Way to go, Canada!" You're finally getting somewhere with that black bastard." I took that as a compliment, and voiced my thanks, as I led Blackjack to his stall.

Donnie said, "We all got worried about you when you didn't come in for supper – thought you were sick or something." She threw her arm around my shoulders. "We've saved your din-din for you. You must be starving."

"Thanks Kiwi," I said. I slipped my arm around her and gave her a squeeze. "You're a good pal."

CHAPTER SIXTEEN

In late November, Mark set up a little
training show for us. It was like a three-
day event with dressage, cross-country
jumping and stadium jumping, but was
held all in one day. He invited riders from
the Taunton and Wellington Hunt Club
and for a week before the show, he was
busy designing and building a jump
course in the outdoor arena. I decided to
ride Blackjack.

Dressage was first, and Blackjack
was horrible. We were only riding a
simple test but it was all I could do to
hold him on a circle, and get him into the
corners. He was nervous with all the
noise and confusion of strange horses
being in the vicinity, and his large dark
eyes darted everywhere except on the
path in front of him. He had a wonderful
floating extended trot when he decided
to use it, but he was too tense and he
didn't reach out with the fluidity I knew
he possessed. On the collected gaits, he
chewed nervously on the bit and tossed
his head far too much. His tail swished in
frustration. Like Redwing, he didn't like
being held in. After receiving our dismal
score, I took him back to his stall and
unsaddled him. Cross-country was after
lunch.

I didn't have time to warm the big black up before we jumped, except for the half-mile ride up to the course. I had ridden him in quiet hacks up here before, and had let him jump some of the smaller ditches and brush jumps. He decided to have a bit of extra fun. We had just started our canter up to the first low jump, when he dropped his shoulder and gave a buck. I was concentrating so hard on the upcoming jump that I was taken completely by surprise, and off I went over his left side, landing hard on my left shoulder and hip. I lay there with the wind knocked out of me while Blackjack, finding himself free, galloped away to a high hill where he had a great view of all the mad scurrying about that he had caused. Quite tickled with himself, he set off again at a gallop leading a merry chase for another mile before he dropped his head to graze and allowed himself to be caught.

By this time I had been helped to the first aid station for evaluation. Fortunately, nothing was broken, but I was bruised and sore. Mark was one of the judges for the day, and had seen me part company with my 'black devil' as he called him.

He came over with a concerned look on his face. "Are ye all right then, Canada?" he asked.

"Yes Sir," I said. "I'm good to go". I
gave him the thumbs up sign. Someone
brought my now thoroughly calm horse
over to me and gave me a leg up. As I
said before, the horses were great
teachers. I had just learned that Blackjack
needed a good gallop before he could
settle down happily to a controlled pace.

He did the course beautifully,
although he tended to go up and down
like a jack-in-a-box. He needed work over
low spreads to make him use his head
and neck and build his confidence. I was
well pleased with him, and realized that
we just needed more time working on his
faults.

In the show jumping arena later
that day I had great hopes that Blackjack
would behave himself. My whole left side
was very stiff and sore, and I was not
looking forward to another battle with
him. In cross-country, although the
ground may be rough with awkward
approaches or a drop upon landing, the
speed of the horse can allow him to use
his head and neck for balance and get out
of trouble. In show jumping, more
accuracy and stability have to be
maintained.

Blackjack trotted into the ring with
his head up and nostrils flaring. It felt like
I was sitting on a keg of dynamite. The
whistle blew signaling me to start. I
kicked him into a canter and just like a

replay of his earlier shenanigans, he corked a buck on the approach to the first jump. This time I was ready for him, and managed to keep my seat as he leapt into the air and came down way off course. He had yanked the reins through my hands, and although I had gloves on, my hands burned. Quickly, I gathered up the extra rein and took a short hold on him, turning him in a circle. My shoulder ached with the sudden jolt he had given me. I took a couple of deep breaths, trying to control my anger and tears. This horse was not going to beat me!

I got a good hold of him, and cantered him in a circle three times. I pleaded with him as the whistle blew again, "Come on, boy, let's just get over the jumps. You don't have to kill me to do it." I saw the worried looks on the faces of the spectators, judges and officials; Liz and Mark among them, as I pointed Blackjack at the course again.

He didn't let me down. He twisted and sprang over every strange obstacle that appeared in front of him. To my delight, he jumped a superbly fast clear round over some tricky fences. The applause we received was well deserved, I thought.

Even more meaningful were Mark's words when we all lined up for the presentations at the end of the day. He came up and pinned a rosette on the lapel of my riding jacket, and said with his Irish eyes smiling, "Good job, Canada!"

Later on when the other girls and I were putting the evening ration into the stalls, Mark appeared with a great load of hay and straw on the barrow. "Hey, Canada," he grinned. "I thought I would give you a hand tonight. You must be sore." He picked up the fork and started to shake out the flakes.

"Thank you, but I'm okay. I can manage," I said, stubbornly. In truth, I was desperately tired and in great pain from my fall today. I wanted nothing else but to soak in a hot tub, take some painkillers, and fall asleep. Mark had other ideas.

He leaned on his fork and watched me, taking in my slow, painful walk and stiff movements. "Hey, Canada," he said softly. "We had a great day today. I'd like to take you out for a decent meal to celebrate. I'm not in the mood for Mrs. Culvers' corned beef and cabbage tonight. How about it?"

"Just me?" I asked stupidly.

Mark rolled his eyes around the stall. "I don't see anyone else standing in here, do you?"

I blushed and stammered, "Oh...I don't think I should. I mean...I don't know if it's allowed. I should hit the sack early tonight. It's been a big day."

Mark just kept on looking at me with the corners of his mouth turned up in a grin. He knew I was embarrassed. "What you do mean, if it's allowed? This is not a bloody prison is it? You are old enough to go out in the evening, are you not?" I shrugged.

"Oh, I get it," Mark said with a laugh. "Liz has warned you fair maidens not to go out with me, hasn't she?"

I squirmed, but met his steady gaze. "She only said not to get involved with the male staff, and apart from Jeremy the half wit, and Joe, who must be ten years older than Liz, you are the only male on staff." I brushed hay chaff off my sleeves. "And besides, I don't have anything to wear to a nice place."

Mark hung the fork on the wall, and turned to me. "Just change out of those muddy togs and let your hair loose, and you'll do fine. I'll clear it with Liz. We won't stay late. I'd just like to go out for a meal, and I'd like to have your company. That's all, okay?"

His Irish lilt went up and down the scale like a Celtic harp, and I loved the sound of it. I felt myself falling under the spell of the Leprechauns as I accepted his offer.

CHAPTER SEVENTEEN

In half an hour I had changed out of my riding clothes and donned a clean pair of jeans, shirt and vest. I released my hair out of the bun it had been stuffed into in order to fit neatly under my riding helmet. I had cut my dark blonde hair to shoulder length and it was naturally curly at the ends. I brushed it out, and put on a little lipstick and blush. When I stepped out of Bredalbane House, Mark was waiting in the red sports car.

We drove to a restaurant Mark knew in Wellington. The front part was a pub, which was busy with noisy patrons, but in back there was a quiet dining room. A buxom waitress appeared at our table. "Something from the bar?" she said.

Mark said, "A pint of draft please, love." And then he looked at me expectantly, and said, "What'll you have Canada?"

"Uh..oh, I don't know, maybe a glass of white wine. I don't usually drink liquor." I felt like a fool.

"Bring a Brandy Alexander for the lady," Mark said to the waitress with a grin, and then to me, he said. "It'll help those bruises and sore muscles."

I grinned back. "You mean, I'll be feeling no pain after I drink one?"

"You catch on quick," he laughed.

The drinks came, and the Brandy Alexander was delicious. I felt it burn in the pit of my empty stomach and then the heat of it spread throughout my limbs. Mark was right; my bruises and aching muscles suddenly felt a lot better!

He ordered steak, baked potatoes, and salad for us both. We sipped our drinks while we waited. Mark leaned forward and looked into my flushed face. "So tell me, Canada, why did you pick that black bastard to ride today when you could have had a fun day on plucky little Chester or one of the mares? They're both bonny jumpers."

I sighed. "I guess I like a challenge, and I did it for Blackjack. He needed the exposure to crowds and excitement and I wanted him to build his confidence in me." I took a sip of my drink. "I just wanted to push him a little today to see what he would do. He has so much potential. He's going to be an awesome jumper."

Mark said, "I would have canned him long ago. You've done wonders with him, lass. You've both come a long way and I'm downright proud of how you handled him and yourself today. You're a real trooper."

"Thanks Mark." I said, feeling pleasure and genuine surprise. He wasn't one to hand out accolades, and this was the second time today that he had praised my accomplishments. I was feeling pretty good myself about making progress with such a difficult horse. It hadn't been an easy day, but I was pleased with the outcome.

The meal came, and as we dug into the tender steak, Mark asked me, "Have you got someone special at home?"

"Yes," I said. "At least, I think so...I have a boyfriend named Russell. We went to school together and we were great friends, but he's mad at me for leaving. He wanted to get married, but I didn't want to settle down yet." I paused, wondering how much I should tell Mark. "I wanted to come over here and get my B.H.S. certificate, so we kind of parted on bad terms. I've written to him three times, but he hasn't answered, so I don't know where I stand with him."

Mark said, "He's a bloody fool. You can't hold a bird when it wants to fly, eh Canada? Has he got horses too?"

"Yes, he lives on a dairy farm, and he has a wonderful buckskin Quarter Horse. Russell is active in high school rodeo. Calf roping is his event."

Mark looked at me thoughtfully. "I've never been to a rodeo," he said. "I may just have to come over to Canada for a visit."

I said something about it being a big country and there being lots to see. Then I asked Mark about his family.

117

"Och, me mam and da are good Irish Catholics (the way he pronounced Catholics was like 'catlicks' and it made me laugh). They went forth and multiplied like the Good Book says, and there's the seven of us to show for it." He took a mouthful of potato and washed it down with ale. "There's Michael, he's the eldest, then Shamus, then myself, Sean, Kathleen, Marie-Celeste, and Lorena. Michael and Kathleen are married with a bunch of little devils between them."

"Wow," I said. "That's quite a clan." I gave him an inquisitive glance, "And are you a good Irish Catlick too?" I asked.

Mark put his tongue firmly in his cheek, and gave me a wink. "Oh well then, I am twenty-eight years old. I have to admit I may have strayed from the fold a wee time or two".

I grinned at him. "A rake and ramblin' boy, I'd say." He grinned back and then looked serious.

"Lindsey Wakefield", he said, looking into my eyes. "Now that's a real British name if I ever heard one. What's your background?"

"Actually, my dad's here in England," I said haltingly. "Only...I haven't seen him for ten years. He left my mom on her own to raise three girls."

Mark was genuinely surprised. He put down his fork. "Your da's over here, and he doesn't even know you're here?"

"That's right." I said. "I've been trying to get up the nerve to call him, but I can't seem to make myself do it. I know I should. I think I'll write to him first to break the ice, so to speak, but I just haven't got around to it yet."

"You should be going there for Christmas. We have a week off, you know." Mark looked at me pointedly.

"I know. I should contact him. But I don't really want to go there for Christmas. I think by Easter, I'll feel more like contacting him. He's married again, and I'm nervous about meeting his new wife. Besides, Donnie and Britt-Marie are going on a tour over Christmas, and they've asked me to go with them. Joan has relatives in Scotland, and she's going to spend Christmas with them."

Mark pushed his empty plate aside, took both of my hands in his, and leaned close over the table. "Come home with me to Ireland for Christmas." His invitation shocked me. I tried to pull my hands away, but he held on, forcing me to look into his deep blue eyes.

"I couldn't do that." I stammered.

"And why not" he insisted. "We've lots of room and me mam and da would love to meet you...as would all my brothers and sisters. Please come."

"But" I protested, "You have such a large family. I wouldn't want to impose. Will they all be home? "

Mark kept holding my hands. I had no choice but to relax and look at him. "I think they'll all be there. And we have a large house – plenty of room. And we have a few ponies to ride. We could go out hacking. The countryside's beautiful. And we'd go out on the Boxing Day Hunt. It's great fun. You'd love it!"

"A real foxhunt?" He nodded. I was definitely interested. "Is your house big, like Bredalbane?" I asked.

"Yeah," he grinned. "Big like Bredalbane. You could have your own room and private bath."

"Really?" I asked. I was getting intrigued. And then I thought of something else.

"Oh Mark," I said, "I don't have any nice clothes to wear, you know, dresses and the like. I only own one skirt. You'd be going to church, and to friend's places and I'd be"--

"Dinna fash yerself about that!" he laughed. My three sisters would have a ball dressing you up. Those girls have more dresses than the Queen of England." I had to laugh too.
Mark ordered Irish coffees to end the meal, and as we enjoyed the nightcap, Mark pretty well talked me into going to Dun Laoghaire where his family farm was.

I sighed and relented. "Well, I guess it is my only chance to see some of Ireland. Maybe it's the drink talking, but I would like to come, that is, if you're sure it's all right with your mother. Won't you have to ask her?"

"I'll *tell* her you're coming. She'll be delighted." We rose and put on our jackets, and went out into the misty night air.

I fell asleep against Mark's broad shoulder soon after we started for Fulmer. He put his arm around me and held me close, letting me sleep until we pulled up at Bredalbane House. He woke me gently and came around to my side to help me out of the car. My mind was in an alcoholic haze coupled with exhaustion and pain from my injured shoulder, and the exciting turn of events that today had generated.

I think I managed to mumble "Goodnight and thank you for a wonderful evening" before I staggered up the stairs to bed.

CHAPTER EIGHTEEN

During Christmas week, the horses were to be turned out in the pastures where only minimal care would be required. Liz and Joe would look after the feeding. There were no stalls to clean. The couple was expecting friends and family to arrive for the holiday, and I think they were looking forward to having the place to themselves for a change

A lot of speculation and excited gossip was exchanged about me going home with Mark for Christmas, but it was soon accepted as everyone became immersed in their own plans for the holiday.

I went into a little funk of depression for a few days; nothing serious, just feeling melancholy about not being home with my own family for Christmas. Then I thought of Mom, over in a strange country with an old lady that was no relation, and of Joan, Donnie and Britt-Marie – all strangers in a strange land.

I cheered up when I got Christmas cards and letters from my sisters, a letter and card from Pam with the news that Redwing was fine and was earning her keep as a lesson horse, and a package and newsy letter from Mom and Victoria in Estoril, Portugal, where they were spending the winter in a posh hotel. Most of the Scottish people we had visited sent a card, and I got a note from Stuart in Oban. A card arrived from the Robson family who were renting our house in Abbotsford. They sent pictures of the kids with Ying-Yang and Buck, and everyone looked happy. I also received a card from Marcie and Ben Livingston, but nothing from Russell.

I didn't have time to brood about him as Mark and I headed north through Gloucester, Birmingham, Derby, Liverpool, and finally into the seaside port of Holyhead where we were to board the ferry for Dublin. The ferry didn't sail until three in the morning, so Mark and I had a leisurely meal in the hotel, and then walked around the old town looking at the many old Roman remains. We boarded the Cambria at nine p.m. and were sound asleep in lounge chairs by ten thirty.

The Cambria docked at seven a.m.and the first thing I noticed was all the signs were in English and Irish Gaelic. I also noted that Ireland seemed to be greener than any other place I'd ever seen. Even in winter, the fields were a beautiful shade of green. It was lovely.

In a short time, we were out of the city and into the surrounding countryside of Bray and the village of Dun Laoghaire.

"How do you get Dun Leary out of Dun Lay-og-hair?" I asked Mark. "Do you speak the Gaelic?" I couldn't see how anyone could get his or her tongue around this language.

Mark slowed the Porsche and swung wide to allow a flock of woolly sheep to pass by. "It's a tough language to learn," he said. "You pretty well have to learn it at your mama's knee. My folks used it when they didn't want us kids to know what they were talking about, so I'm not fluent in it. I understand most of what is said, but I have trouble speaking it."

We were approaching an entranceway with towering oak trees on either side of the driveway. When Mark turned in, I could see a metal plate on the stone wall that read: Leamaneh: McTaggart Estates. Est. 1852. I took in the view of manicured green pastures bordered by endless white fences. That in itself was very odd here, as most pasture divisions were made of stones that had been laboriously picked from the fields. We passed a couple of small stone cottages, and then as we rounded a corner, there on a wide expanse of manicured lawns and gardens, stood an immense castle with four turrets. A large stone coach house stood at the end of a curving lane, and I could see quite a number of horses grazing in the fields.

I was speechless for a moment, and then I found my voice. "Oh my God, Mark! You didn't tell me you lived in a humongous castle! Is this *really* your place?"

"Yep," he grinned. He was enjoying himself immensely, watching shock and surprise settle over me. " At least I'll inherit one seventh of it some day. He looked over at me shyly. "Maybe I forgot to tell you that my da owns a big distillery. You not being much of a drinker, you probably haven't heard of McTaggart Whisky." I shook my head. I just sat there staring, too stunned to get out of the car. Two great Irish wolfhounds circled around us, barking their heads off. Mark rolled the window down and spoke to them. "Here Mischief, here Trouble, come!" The dogs galloped over and reared up on their hind legs, while shoving their big heads in the window to lick Mark's face. "All right, get down, that's enough," he yelled. "Come on Canada, let's go and meet the family."

I took a deep breath and followed Mark and the exuberant dogs up the stone stairs to the massive front door. Once inside, it was total chaos. People descended on us from all areas of the huge living areas. I was met and hugged by Maureen, Mark's mom, his 'da,' Michael Sr., and all the siblings and their children. There were about six kids

running around and in the noise and
confusion, I wasn't sure who belonged to
whom.

The noisy throng led us through
the great hall past a wide oak staircase to
the back kitchen where two maids were
busy preparing and serving breakfast.
Suddenly I was hungry. Fresh-baked
scones, marmalade, platters of fried eggs
and sausages were passed around the
table while the maids topped up the
coffee cups. Marks's mom reminded me
of a younger version of Mrs. Donnelly.
She had those same kind of violet-blue
eyes, her skin was clear and smooth like
that of a baby, and her auburn hair was
just going silver at the temples. For a
woman that had raised seven children she
looked remarkably young. I was seated
next to her and across from Mark, where
she kept us both engaged in lively
conversation. Michael Sr. was at the head
of the table. He looked to be ten or
twelve years older than Maureen. His hair
and moustache were white, his eyes a
vivid blue, and his somewhat large nose
was rather red, showing the effects of the
whisky he sampled daily to test the
quality of the product he produced.

After breakfast, Mark and I brought
in our bags from the car and he led me
up the grand staircase, down a very long
hallway carpeted in red, to a hexagon-
shaped room in the west wing. I felt like I

was in a very posh hotel. The large
canopy bed was covered with a pale
purple silk bedspread. When I placed my
backpack on the bed, it looked very out
of place. A peat fire had been laid in the
fireplace, ready to be lit whenever I
wanted it. I walked over to one of the
large windows, which had a view of
rolling green hills, woods and a distant
stream. "This is wonderful," I said. "How
did your family come to live in a castle,
Mark? And what does the name mean?"

"Leamaneh?" It's Irish for 'stag
leaps' or 'horses leap'. There have been
horses here since Norman times, back in
the thirteenth century. The O'Connor's
built it, but they were chased out when
Cromwell invaded Ireland and then it
changed hands several times as the clan
wars raged. My ancestors have lived here
continuously since 1852. It's been
constantly restored and updated.

""How much land is there?" I asked,
still gazing at the view from the window.

"There are 350 acres of woods and
meadows," he replied. There are fifteen
bedrooms, and ten of them have their
own bathrooms attached. Yours is just
through the door there", he indicated
with a nod of his head. There's the back
kitchen where we had breakfast, the
formal dining room, where by the way,
supper will be served at 6 p.m.
Ah...there's a ballroom, a music room, a

huge library, a conservatory, a suite of offices relating to the business, there's a wine cellar, a sauna, and a couple of . playrooms for the kids. I'll give you a tour later on. Would you like to go out and see the horses now?"

I had already had a glimpse of the rich paneling on the walls, the intricate woodcarvings, the old works of art and the antique furniture, but mention of seeing the horses caught my attention.

"Yes, of course!" I enthused. I always wanted to look at horses.

We walked down the winding path to the coach house and what Mark had told me were his 'few ponies' turned out to be a stable full of the most beautiful Irish Hunters I had ever seen. The barn was more luxurious than most people's houses. A couple of stable hands were working in the barn, and they greeted Mark with handshakes and smiles. I could see he was well liked. We stopped in front of one of the big box stalls. "Hello Merlin, you big oaf," Mark said to the tall chestnut that stuck his head out for attention. Mark held the big horse's face in his hands and gave the rubbery nose a resounding kiss. "Did ye miss me boy?" and then, "Has he been behavin' Paddy?"

"Oh aye Sir," the groom called Paddy said. "Ee's in right good form. ee's been 'unting regular, Sir"

"Excellent Paddy. Would you saddle
him up for me? And what do you have in
for the lady here? She's a crack rider."

"Well then," said Paddy with a big
smile. I could tell he was an old ex
jockey, probably steeplechase. He was
very short and his legs were bandy and
bowlegged. He walked with a limp, which
I surmised was probably an old horse
related injury.

We walked along to a stall down the
row, and Paddy slid the metal door open.
"Come 'eer pet," he said softly. Then to
me, he said, "I think you might know this
mare." I stared at her with interest. She
was dappled gray with a dark mane and
tail, and had the loveliest, softest eyes I
had ever seen on a horse since...Desert
Fire. I stroked the mare on her fine silky
neck and she turned and snuffed me
gently. "I'm sure I don't know her, but
she looks exactly like a young one I have
at Fulmer." Paddy and Mark exchanged
glances and grins.

"Would 'is name be Desert Fire,
Miss?" Paddy asked. I looked up, startled.

"How would you know that?"

He and Mark started to laugh.
"Because this is Desert Wind, 'is mama."

"What?" I said. "No wonder they
look so much alike.That's amazing! So,
why is he at Fulmer?"

Mark answered for me. "Well, you
see, we send our colts out to the various

equestrian centers for training. We find the students do a good job on starting them, and they're usually sold at the end of the year. It's a way to get the young ones trained and marketed. And, since I was going to be teaching at Fulmer this year, we decided to send Desert Fire there.

"So," Paddy, said, "You've been training our 'orse for us. 'Ow is ee doing?"

"Oh, I love him!" I said. "He is so easy to train. He lunges and ground drives beautifully bitted up to the surcingle, and he's had the saddle on a couple of times. I'm going to start riding him after Christmas. He's a lovely horse, so beautiful and kind." I gave Mark a playful poke in the arm. "Why didn't you tell me he was your horse? You're just full of surprises, aren't you?"

Mark grinned. "That's the way of the Irish. Just like the fairies – we like to play tricks on people!"

CHAPTER NINETEEN

For the next couple of days, Mark and I went riding around the estate – he on Merlin, and I on Desert Wind. With various members of the family, we also tried our hand at archery, tennis, golf, and fishing. I loved to walk around the rose gardens with its many fountains. Of course the roses weren't blooming in December, but in the greenhouse there were many flowering shrubs and plants. It was difficult to imagine all the trouble one always heard about in Ireland when there was nothing but peace, happiness, and beauty at Leamaneh.

We went to the church for midnight mass on Christmas Eve. I found the Catholic service a little different than what I was used to, but I enjoyed the choir music and the timeless message of Jesus' birth. Christmas Day was great fun with a lot of feasting, games, and music, and a treasure hunt around the castle. I was happy to see that the family favored togetherness over expensive gifts that nobody needed.

.   On Boxing Day Mark knocked on my door early in the morning. "Canada! Are ye up lass?" he yelled.

"Yes...coming!" I called out." *It couldn't possibly be time to get up.* I thought. Then I remembered – the hunt! I was going on a foxhunt!

Down at the stable, Paddy mounted me on Fitzroy, a solid bay, rather short-legged gelding. "We're not taking Desert Wind out on hunts just now as she is in foal," he smiled up at me. This fellow is not particularly fast, but 'ees clever and full of stamina. 'Ee's great at jumping various angles, and I think you'll find 'ee's your best choice."

"You know your horses, Paddy," I smiled back at him. "He'll do just fine, thanks."

I joined Mark who was riding the feisty Merlin. About fifteen riders, mounted on their Thoroughbreds and wearing white leathers, top hats and pink coats exuded a great aura of expensiveness as they gathered around the Hunt Master. A small glass of sherry, called a 'stirrup cup' was passed around from a silver platter. The drink was meant to ward off the morning mists and chill. I noticed later on that many riders carried a silver flask in their saddle pouches or coat pockets, (no doubt containing McTaggart whisky) and some of these riders ended up falling from their horses. Mark raised his glass to me. "Sla'inte chugat Canada!" he said. "Enjoy your hunt!" All around me I heard the same toast being given and also "Mora na maidine dhuit" (Top of the morning to you.)

The tricolored foxhounds yapped and pawed frantically at the wire doors of their kennels while the Huntsman explained the rules. "No passing the Hunt Master, keep your horse and yourself quiet when hounds are drawing or at a check; avoid giving the Huntsman unnecessary information, give the Huntsman and his hounds plenty of room, never crack your whip at a hound and never hit a hound, always turn your horses head towards them, and always offer your horse to the Huntsman if his goes lame or loses a shoe."

That little speech being said, he lifted the brass horn that was tied to his saddle and blasted a few notes on it. Then he yelled "Tallyho!" The kennel staff released the hounds and we were all off at a mad gallop.

Merlin soon outdistanced my little Fitzroy, but I didn't mind just cantering along easily. He jumped like a deer, be it ditches, brush, or fence, and I soon began to just enjoy watching the hounds work and the beauty of the countryside. I secretly hoped we wouldn't find a real fox for I didn't want to see the hounds kill it. Mark had told me earlier that the fox enjoys the chase too, and will often turn aside to kill a mouse, rat, frog or rabbit. They seldom seemed to show any sign of agitation until very near the end of a long hunt and then not for very long, fortunately.

This day, Mr. Reynard was fortunate, for although the hounds put one up and a strenuous and exhilarating chase followed, he managed to outwit all those keen noses and go to ground before we caught up to him.

It was a great day, from the start at the stables, to the coffee and ham sandwiches that miraculously appeared at lunchtime, to the return; muddy, hungry, but happy in the twilight. It left an indelible picture on my mind, and even a wet, blank day with a north wind blowing through my ribs couldn't have deterred me from enjoying the hunt.

The day before we left Leamanah, Mark and I were out hacking around the many beautiful trails on the estate. There had been showers all morning, but the afternoon was clear and bright. Raindrops reflected the sunshine like tiny jewels on the grass, trees and shrubs. Everything smelled fresh and clean. We'd been for a brisk canter and when I caught up to Mark's Merlin, my cheeks were rosy. As I came alongside, Mark leaned over and put his arm around me. I turned toward him in surprise, which is exactly what he wanted me to do. He planted a kiss on my lips, and then he let me go. "Begorah!"

he said, smiling. "You just look so bonny
- so alive - I just had to kiss you!"

To hide my embarrassment, I
kicked Desert Wind into a canter again. In
a flash the big chestnut was alongside.
"You're not mad at me, are you Canada?"
he asked. I slowed Desert Wind to a walk.

"No, of course not." I grinned at
him. "There's no harm in a friendly kiss."

Mark seemed pleased. He said,
"There's a ceilidh tonight at the Roisn
Dubh. Would you like to go? It's great
fun. There's singing and dancing, and of
course lots of drinking. Sean and Lorena
want to go as well." He looked at me
hopefully.

"Sure," I said. That sounds fine."

Back at the castle, I stopped at Lorena's
room to see what she was going to wear
for the dance, and to ask if I could
borrow an outfit for the evening. She
looked at me shyly, her dark eyes dancing
with mischief. "Go and have a look on
your bed. There's a wee giftie from Mark
for you. He had me do a little shopping
today." When I hesitated, she shooed me
out, saying "Go on!"

Puzzled, yet curious, I went to
check it out, and there, laid out on my
bed against the purple satin cover, was a
red velvet dress in exactly my size. The
neckline was low cut, the sleeves short
and the bodice snug fitting with the skirt

billowing out. Beside the dress was a little jewelry box containing a pearl necklace. I had no idea if the pearls were real or not, but they shimmered with iridescence and beauty when I held them up to the light.

Lorena was just a year and a half older than I. She was so beautiful with her dark eyes, olive skin, and naturally curly thick hair. Mark told me that the fairies had stolen his mother's redheaded daughter at birth and replaced her with this Gypsy child. Sometimes he was so full of the blarney I didn't know what to believe!

When Lorena and I came down the wide, oak stairs a little later, dolled up like two princesses, Mark just stood there speechless staring at us. Then, as Sean started down the stairs behind us, he shouted to him, "Sean! Fetch me my sunglasses! I'm fairly dazzled by the radiant beauty of these two lasses." We all burst into laughter at his nonsense. Mark looked very handsome too. He wore his army dress uniform, which consisted of white breeches, brown leather boots, a white shirt, and a red tunic with brass buttons and gold tassels on the shoulders. The four of us squeezed into the small sports car and with Sean singing Irish ballads in the back seat, we were off to the Ceilidh.

I'd never been to such a dance! Ooh, the Irish people love their music and history, along with copious amounts of whisky to tell of it. Fiddles and accordions, drums, bagpipes and Irish whistles all made a lovely noise. I danced reels and jigs, polkas and waltzes with, I am sure, every able bodied man in the house. They all wanted a turn round the dance floor with the Canadian lass. Mark was drinking McTaggart Whisky. With glass in hand, he got up and sang 'The Oak and the Ash' and on every chorus everyone joined in loudly with "And it's home, boys, home!" (clap.clap.) Then he launched into 'Danny Boy'. I knew that one, so I joined him and sang the harmony. We got a great hand. I got so hot dancing that I actually downed a pint or two (who was counting?) of dark, lovely Guinness. I hadn't had a chance all night to thank Mark for the wonderful gift of the dress and the pearls, not to mention all the adventure I was having.

By the time we left for Leamaneh, Sean was falling down drunk and the rest of us were fairly tipsy to say the least. Sean was a great singer, even drunk, as he serenaded us with all the verses of 'Carrickfergus.' We all joined in on the line... 'I'm drunk today, and I'm seldom sober...a handsome rover from town to town...'

The brother and sister disappeared to their beds the instant we got inside the massive oak doors.

"Are ye hungry, Canada?" Mark asked.

"Oh aye, I could use a bittie morsel," I said, trying to mimic his Celtic accent.

"You go on up then, and get comfortable by the fire. I'll bring up a tray with something."

I went up the red-carpeted stairway, down the long empty hallway to my room at the end. The fire had been burning, but was now reduced to coals. I added wood a little at a time until it flared up. I pulled the settee up to the fire and kicked off my shoes. In a few moments Mark was back with a tray with two coffees (Irish of course) and some Irish soda bread and cheese. We had put out a lot of energy dancing and were hungry. While we ate, I tried to think of the right words to say to Mark to thank him for his generous gifts and for sharing his Christmas holidays with me by having me as a guest in his home. "Mark," I said, fingering the pearls around my neck. "These pearls... they look very valuable, and I am just blown away that you would give me such a gift. They're absolutely beautiful, and I thank you very much for them, and also this lovely dress."

Mark took the empty plates and set them on the side table and then he put his arm around me and pulled me to him. He stroked my cheek gently and then he tipped my face up to his and kissed me. I tasted the smoky whiskey; inhaled the smell of his skin, the faint orange-blossom aroma of his expensive aftershave. I thought fleetingly of Russell, but he was far away, and this handsome, generous man was here; touching me, kissing me, and it felt good. Mark pulled the combs from my hair, and my blond tresses fell around my shoulders. He slipped his hands under my hair and unclasped the necklace, holding it in his hand.

"Lindsey," he said solemnly, (for once he didn't call me Canada) "These are genuine pearls; just like you. You are *so* beautiful and natural. It's been a joy having you here this week with me. You're so easy to entertain. You're a good sport about trying new things and you're interested in everything. You're a gem, and I wanted to get you something lasting."

"But, they're so expensive." I protested. "I can't" - He put his fingers against my lips.

"Hush!" he said. "We won't speak of it. In case you haven't noticed, our family is *very* wealthy. I haven't spent my money on anything as satisfying in a long time. So please, just enjoy them."

I flung my arms around him in a genuine hug. "Thank you" I whispered against his ear. "I'll treasure them always."

I guess what happened next was inevitable. Mark unzipped my dress and led me to the huge bed. I thought of saying 'no' but what could I do? I was a guest in his home. I had ridden his best horses, sat at table with his family, shared laughter, music and drink, and been the recipient of his generous gifts. Besides being more than a bit drunk which no doubt clouded my will power, I really liked Mark and I wanted him at that moment as much as he wanted me.

CHAPTER TWENTY

In the morning, I was dimly aware of Mark getting up and leaving the room, but I slept on. I heard the wind and rain pounding on the windows like angry demons. Whenever I moved, my head hurt, and I knew I was suffering a hangover. I had no wish to get up.

About mid morning, there was a polite knock on my door before it opened. I cracked one eye open to see Teresa, the kitchen maid enter with a silver tray. "Sorry to bother you Miss," she said timidly. "Master Mark sent me up with this. He says your head might be a bit wonky this morning."

"Thank you Teresa," I said. " I'm no match for an Irishman when it comes to the drink." She laughed, as she put the tray down on the bed table. "Drink this, and you'll feel better."

When she had closed the door behind her, I sat up and looked at the contents of the tray. The first thing I noticed was a beautiful red rose with little droplets of rain on it lying alongside a large glass of orange juice, a pot of tea, sugar and cream, and two plain scones. Tucked under the napkin, was a note from Mark. I took a long swig of the juice and opened the envelope. It read:
"Good Morning!

I hope you slept well. You missed breakfast. If you need me, the family is having a meeting in the Library this morning. Come in if you want, but it will be financial stuff to do with the business and not very interesting for you – Be ready to leave at noon. Love, Mark
.

I drank the tea and ate the scones while contemplating where on earth Mark had got such a perfect rose at this time of year. I wrapped it gently in wet tissue paper and put it stem first into an outside pocket of my backpack. Then I went and had a leisurely soak in the tub. Even with the central heating I found the castle rooms cold. I could not imagine living here in ancient times with only a peat fire for warmth. No wonder people only bathed occasionally. It was too cold!

Reluctantly emerging from the hot tub, I dressed in jeans, shirt, and woolen sweater. I didn't want to intrude on the family, but I was glad Mark had told me where they all were. The place seemed so huge and quiet without the usual bustle and activity. To pass the time, I donned my rain slicker, boots and a hat and went down to the stables to say goodbye to Paddy and the horses.

I found Paddy polishing saddles in the tack room. "Hi Paddy," I said, coming in from the freezing rain. "Ooh, that's a nasty weather system out there today!"

The little man looked up from his polishing. "Aye," he said. "I hope you're a good sailor. The Irish Sea will be wild today, I fear."

Oh great. I hadn't thought of that. "Well, actually, I still feel a bit queasy from last night," I said, sitting on a box across from Paddy. "I was at the ceilidh last night, and I'm not much of a drinker. I just got so hot with the dancing and all, I got carried away with the Guinness."

Paddy's blue eyes twinkled as he regarded me evenly. "Ah well, you'll have some great memories to take back to Canada when you go."

"That I will, Paddy. And I'd like to thank you for letting me ride Desert Wind and Fitzroy. I had a wonderful time on the hunt and on our rides out on the estate."

"T'ink nothing of it, lass," Paddy smiled. "Its great to have someone like yourself dat knows a t'ing or two about 'orses." I was intrigued by Paddy's way of speaking. He always left the 'h's out of his speech.

We shook hands, and I left him there whistling to himself, as I went down the shed row to say goodbye to Desert Wind. I gave the mare a hug and told her I would be seeing her son shortly. I praised her for her beauty and gentleness and thanked her for taking me on some wonderful rides. As I was leaving the stall, Merlin stuck his big Irish head out of his box stall, demanding attention, so I had to go over and give him a big kiss and hug too.

The lashing rain and wind threatened to tear the clothes off my body as I made my way back into the castle. I went up to my room and packed my meager belongings into my bag. I wondered if I would ever see Leamaneh again.

After a quick light lunch and many tearful goodbyes with promises to keep in touch, Mark and I headed out for Dublin and the ferry to Liverpool. We hadn't had a chance to talk about last night, and with the poor driving conditions and haste to get to the boat on time, I figured that now wasn't a good time. Once on board the heaving ship, I immediately felt sick, and had to run to the ladies' room to get rid of my lunch.

For the next four hours, the ship plunged through one of the roughest seas in thirty years. I stood on deck for a while watching with fascinated horror as we went down, down, down, into a huge trough of dark, sinister water. Just as I thought the monster wave would engulf the whole ship, she turned absolutely perpendicular and climbed up the mountain of water, only to come crashing down on the other side. I was sure we were all going to a watery grave! I clung to Mark in abject misery and fear. He seemed to love the salt spray in his face and the wildness of the wind and waves, but he had the decency not to tease me about my apprehension.

As we drove off the heaving ramp onto solid ground, I burst into praise for God, St. Christopher (the patron saint of travelers), Jesus, Mother Mary, St. Patrick, and any other angels or saints that happened to be listening. Mark nearly went into hysterics laughing at my obvious relief. I still didn't feel very well, so I climbed over into the narrow back seat, pulled my coat over me, and promptly fell asleep for a couple of hours.

I awoke when Mark drove into a hotel parking lot in the early evening. Darkness had descended and thankfully, the rain had stopped. "Come on, Canada," he said, "Let's get something to eat."

I was still kind of groggy and cold as Mark helped me out of the cramped quarters of the small car and into the warmth and light of the restaurant, but I felt better when I had freshened up in the loo. I joined him at the table. "Sorry, I haven't been very good company," I said, slipping into the seat across from him.

He gave me a sympathetic smile. "It's okay. You needed to sleep off the effects of that wild crossing, and no doubt the drink from the night before."

"Yes..."I agreed, studying the menu. "I can still feel the motion of the ship. I don't think I want to go across the sea to Ireland for a while. Whoever wrote that song about Galway Bay must have crossed on a calm day."

Mark grinned. "Yeah...in winter that old channel can get pretty rough. That's one of the wildest crossings I've ever been on, and I've crossed many times." Then, changing the subject he said, "Would you like the roast beef and Yorkshire puddings?"

"Yes, that sounds wonderful." I said. "And trifle for dessert. I am hungry!"

"Me too," Mark said. "I could eat the arse out of a skunk!"

I almost spewed my mouthful of water across the table as I burst out laughing. Mark's expressions, although somewhat crude, had a way of making me giggle. We kept to small talk as we polished off the roast beef dinners and dessert.

Back in the car, Mark reached out and took my hand, lacing his fingers with mine. "Are ye angry with me, Lindsey?" he asked. We had just shared a delightful dinner and light conversation, so I was puzzled.

"No," I said. "Why do you ask?"

Mark looked uncomfortable. "Well..."he said with a shrug. "I thought that since ...you know...I took your virginity, you might be disappointed. Maybe you wanted to keep it for your Canadian cowboy."

"Oh..." I said, trying not to smile too much. "No, I'm not sorry about that." I took a big breath and blew it out audibly. "All the bells and whistles went off, and it was great, but I *am* a bit disappointed that I was almost too drunk to participate." I looked at him sideways. "Perhaps we'll have to try it again when I'm sober."

He pulled me to him then, and tenderly kissed my lips. I stayed where I was, snuggled against him. He kept his arm around me, and his face wore a silly grin as he eased the Porsche out onto the highway. He was immensely pleased with himself.

After a while, I asked him, "Mark, how will we handle this when we get back? Liz warned us girls not to get involved with you."

"Yeah, I know. We'll have to be careful. There's to be no misconduct at Fulmer. You'll still have to call me 'Sir' in your riding lessons, and don't, for God's sake, tell any of the other girls that you've been intimate with me. It'll get us both into trouble."

"I won't," I agreed. I knew they'd be on me like inquisitive cats the moment I stuck my head in the door.

"Where do we go from here?" I
asked. I was beginning to think about the
consequences of our actions. "There's no
future in it, is there? It's just love 'em and
leave 'em. Isn't that how it works?"

Mark sighed and removed his arm
from around my shoulders. "Jaysus!
You're cynical, Canada." He was quiet for
a moment.

Then, he said, softly. "What did you
expect? My life is here. You're going
home to your cowboy. We're attracted to
one another so we might as well enjoy
each other's company while it lasts.
There's no harm done."

We were both pretty quiet after
that. When we neared the entrance to
Fulmer, Mark stopped the car on the side
of the road and took me in his arms,
almost smothering me with kisses. "I'll
leave it up to you, Canada," he whispered
in my ear. "If you want to end it now, I'll
respect that. But, by the Jaysus, I'd like to
take you to bed right this minute."

We spent ten minutes just kissing
and holding each other. I knew it would
not be the end, but just the beginning of
something wild and wonderful.

CHAPTER TWENTY-ONE

There was a lot of excited chatter the next morning during chores and at breakfast, as we all got caught up on each other's adventures over Christmas break. Of course the girls were dying to know how my Irish trip went, and they were totally amazed to hear that Mark's family lived in a huge castle. I told them about the Boxing Day Hunt, and that Desert Fire's dam had been my riding horse at the estate. "So you see, the McTaggarts have an interest in me – because I'm training their horse. That's why Mark invited me to go home with him."

Joan put her hands on her hips and struck a jaunty pose. "And I suppose it has nothing to do with your gorgeous blond hair and saucy blue eyes!"

I shrugged and laughed. "I don't think so, Joan. *You* can have him. He's too old for me." We punched each other playfully, and got on with mucking the stalls.

If we thought we were busy before Christmas, we were in for a surprise for the next term. Of course we were now more efficient at doing our chores. As well as riding our young horses under Mark's supervision, we were surprised to learn that he was also our teacher for a unit on nutrition and vet care. Whenever the vets came to do any procedures, we were required to pay close attention, but Mark also taught us how to bandage legs and tails; how to take a horse's temperature, pulse and respiration, how to give shots, and doctor small wounds. Likewise when the farrier came to trim or shoe, we all took a turn donning the heavy leather apron and learning how to use the nippers and rasp. Mark taught us about feed rations; calcium to phosphorous balances, proteins, and additives such as salt and minerals and how they affected a horses health and performance. We had to pay attention, as we were tested, graded and evaluated on each unit. None of us had any spare time. By the end of the week, I was very much looking forward to my day off.

A leisurely bath was first on my list. Then while my laundry was drying, I wrote to Russell, telling him everything about my Irish trip, except of course that I had slept with Mark. I still checked the mail every day, hoping for a letter from him.

After lunch, I took the bus into Taunton. I wanted to mail my letter, and restock my stash of oranges, chocolate biscuits, and licorice. If we were to work without breakfast, I made darn sure I had a snack in my pockets to munch on. I had also discovered that Blackjack loved licorice, and I used it to bribe him to come to me on command by kissing to him, and rewarding him with a piece. He would close his eyes and munch with a look of ecstasy on his face while black drool dribbled from his lips. I was becoming his buddy.

Coming out of the grocer's in Taunton with my purchases, I wasn't too surprised to hear a familiar voice behind me say, "Would you be needin' a lift somewhere, Missy?" I turned to see Mark standing beside his car with the door open. I slid into the expensive leather seat with my heart racing. "Yes sir," I grinned. "That would be great."

Once on the road, I asked him, "How did you get away? I thought you were teaching this afternoon."

"I was," he smiled as he reached for my hand. "I sent them out on a training ride." We headed west, with the powerful car eating up the miles. Mark was in a hurry to put some distance between the village and anyone who might recognize us.

In a half hour we were passing the ruins of an old Abbey on a twisty back road which ran between the ranks of towering oak, elm and beech trees. We came to a high, crumbling stone wall that must have been impressive in its day, but was now broken in places by huge branches that had come down in the wind. Ivy and holly sprawled out of

control in a tangle between the cracks. Mark eased the Porsche into an almost hidden driveway. You would have to know it was there in order not to miss it.
"Where are we?" I asked, looking around in wonder.

"Welcome to Thornhylde, my hideaway."

"You *own* this?" I asked. I could just see the slate-gray of the rooftop thick with dark green moss and lichen peeking out of the tangle of thorn hedge. The house that stood behind a small wicket gate, once painted white, was stone-built, and well proportioned with long narrow windows, and a solid red door with an old brass (now green with age) horse head door knocker.

Mark must have planned this, for he had hired a man to go in earlier and light the fires, When we entered and hurried straight up the wide, shallow stairs to the broad landing and into a large bedroom on the south side, the house was surprisingly comfortable.

When we came down to the kitchen an hour later, flushed and giddy with lovemaking, we found tea things laid out; cold meat, butter and bread, sugar and a half bottle of milk.

"So you bought this, just so we could have a place to meet secretly?" I asked. I was incredulous that he would go to such lengths so we would not be discovered. I took a bite of my bread and butter and waited for an answer.

Mark stirred his tea and looked at me dreamily. His reddish-brown hair was still all mussed up. His shirt was open at the collar and his riding jods had been replaced with an old pair of jeans. His feet were bare. He looked so cute and boyish – so different from the arrogant, stern riding instructor that barked orders at me in my riding lessons. I was beginning to see another side of him, which I liked very much. He could be sweet and gentle and he was certainly generous. I got up and went around to his side of the table and climbed onto his knee and put my arms around him. I wished we did not have to leave. It would be fun to stay here in this old house with him, fix up the yard and garden, and have our horses grazing in the nearby orchard...my mind drifted off in dreams until Mark spoke, bringing me back to the present. "I bought it for an investment," he said, running his hand up and down my back. "I'm going to get it fixed up and will probably sell it in a year or two. Or maybe I'll keep it; it's an interesting old place."

"It sure is," I agreed. I'd love to explore the grounds, but I guess there isn't time. Don't you have to be back at four thirty for Pony Club?"

Mark nodded. "Yep. We'd better get going. I'll have to drop you at the bus stop in Taunton, and go on alone. Sorry about that." He gave me a kiss and stood up. "Let's go."

We got our few things together, checked the fires, and closed the door on Thornhylde.

Our meetings were to be few and far between. Mark's schedule and mine were often in conflict, and as spring approached, the work increased on the farm so that sometimes our days off were reduced to a couple of hours to do our laundry or go for a sleep. We were on foal watch at night. Princess Valentine and Polly Royal had been brought down to the foaling stalls. All of us, including Liz took turns checking the mares for imminent signs of giving birth. These horses were too valuable to be left to their own devices.

We also started at this time to teach our own students that came for lessons on the weekends or evenings. We had to have a lesson plan approved by Mark, and we had to follow it in our teaching. We couldn't just wing it or make something up on the spot. Mark evaluated us on our performance. At first, I found it very hard to teach with him watching, but I soon learned to ignore him and follow my lesson plans.

Depending on our schedules, Liz also took us in turns with her to the office to learn the business side of managing a horse farm. We practiced typing, and each kept a set of identical ledgers, tracking the expenses and income on the farm. She got us to do the phone orders for bedding, feed, and vet supplies. I grew to have a lot of respect for all that Liz and Joe did on the farm. We didn't see much of Joe, but his presence was evident in the manicured gardens, fresh shavings in the pens, a tractor and farm truck that had regular maintenance, and fences that were kept painted.

I found out that Liz had a degree in Business Management, and had worked for government officials in London before taking on the job as manager at Fulmer. One day at afternoon tea, I asked her why she had traded in her nine to five job in a posh office to come and work a twelve to fourteen hour day with recalcitrant horses and young ladies that didn't know a coronet band from a trumpet when they started.

She got a faraway look in her gray eyes as she pushed her untidy hair back off her face. "You know...I have dresses in my closet that I haven't worn for years. I have matching shoes and handbags that

I'll never use again." She shook her head. "No, I'll never go back to that phony existence. Out here, if I forget to order the feed or bedding, or if I don't call the vet when a horse is injured, or having trouble foaling, those horses that are depending on me will suffer. And horses are such honest and noble creatures. I do it for them. And I like to work with you girls because you want to be here too; you respect and love the countryside and the horses. You're learning the value of honesty and hard work. There's nothing quite like the feeling of knowing you have done a good day's work. It's way better than putting together the perfect deal and then going for coffee to talk about the poor jerk you just double-crossed, all the while worrying about your hair and your make-up and whether or not you have a run in your stocking." Liz drained her cup and stood up. She looked somewhat embarrassed that a simple question had turned into a speech. "Come on – let's get to work."

Desert Fire was coming along beautifully under saddle. Joan, Donnie, Britt-Marie and I all rode our young horses in a lesson with Mark right after morning chores. After a month of arena work, Mark said we could start alternating arena work with short hacks out on the cross-country course. I started popping Desert

Fire over small jumps and ditches. He was a natural jumper and very easy to handle. I was going to be sorry to see him go when he was sold.

My other young horse, Monty, was to be the mount of a twelve-year-old boy that had outgrown his Welsh/Shetland cross. Tony was a keen rider working his way through the Pony Club levels. He came for lessons on Monty, and in no time he could handle the young animal like a pro. I had no qualms about seeing them go off together on a ride. They were going to make a great team. Mark released Monty from the program with high praise for the job I had done on breaking the pony to saddle. I felt pretty good about my first graduate.

With Monty gone, that left me a little more time to work on Blackjack. His owner, Mr. Symes, came over from time to time to watch the training sessions. I said to him, " I always lunge him for at least twenty minutes before I get on him. He'll fool around for the first five minutes, bucking and tossing his head, and he'll likely kick the wall if you're too close to the edge of the arena. He's quite a character." I had showed Mr. Symes how I could now catch the gelding out in his paddock easily and how his stall manners had improved. He was so impressed that he slipped me a five pound note when he left, and said, "Keep up the good work." I

was starting to feel pretty good about my
horse training abilities.

CHAPTER TWENTY-TWO

I got to see my first foal being born when Princess Valentine went into labor. Liz came and shook me awake at five in the morning. She had the video monitor on in her bedroom, which was hooked up to the foaling stall so she knew immediately when the action started. I dressed quickly and quietly so as not to disturb the other girls. We would all get chances to watch the foals being born, and to help, as was sometimes necessary.

As we approached the stall, we could hear the mare's restless movements and sense her agitation. We slipped into the stall quietly. Liz spoke gently to the mare and held her by the halter while I bandaged the tail as Mark had taught us. This wasn't necessary, Liz told me, but helped to keep it from being matted with afterbirth and blood. Then we waited and watched from outside the stall. The pretty dark bay mare paced in circles around the stall, pawing at the bedding, flopping down and then almost immediately getting up again. This went on for a few minutes, and then as she turned in a circle, I could see that she had 'presented'. There was a large white looking bubble under her tail, and I could just make out the shape of two tiny hooves with a nose tucked between.

159

"Good lass," sighed Liz. "It's coming the right way. It won't be long now. It's a bugger when they come backwards".

I looked at her in surprise. I had never heard her swear before. "What happens then?" I asked her.

"Well, it's a whole lot of very hard work, for the mare and for us trying to help. You have to pull the foal, and it almost always drowns in its own fluid. It's not a pretty sight." Liz crossed her arms and shook her head. "No, if you raise horses, sooner or later, you'll lose a few. It's always hard." Then she smiled. "But this one's alive! There she goes!" Princess Valentine's knees buckled and then her rump and body collapsed on the straw. She grunted and pushed hard a couple of times, and then, in a mass of blood and fluid, the amniotic sac slid out.

"This is your first foaling girl," Liz said. "Get in there and break the sac. It usually breaks itself, but sometimes it doesn't so it's good to be here so the little tykes don't suffocate."

I knelt quickly and pulled the thick, sticky membrane away from the foal's face. Princess Valentine nickered softly; her head turned to look at her new baby. The tiny, dark, wet head wavered and lifted; then his whole body wiggled and the rest of him slid out. The morning air was chilly; making steam rise off the

warm, wet body. Liz popped in and
squatted beside me. She lifted a hind leg
on the foal, and said, "It's a colt."

I just couldn't stop staring at the
perfect little horse. Liz put a hand on my
shoulder. "Back up a bit now, she's going
to get up."

As I stood up, the mare lunged to
her feet also, and spun around to have a
look at the colt. She made funny little
grunts and squeals deep in her throat.
"Baby talk." I laughed.

"Yes," Liz said, smiling. "She's
communicating with her baby. You can
just hear the joy in her voice. And see,
when she turned like that, the umbilical
cord broke. I've seen mares bite it off, if
it doesn't break by itself."

"Wow!" I marveled. "That's
amazing."

We got out of the way and let the
mare bond with her new baby. She
pushed him with her nose. She nickered
to him, and she began to lick him all over
with great swipes of her raspy tongue. I
laughed out loud at the high-pitched little
whinny he answered with. As the colt
began to dry off, we could see that he
was a dark bay like his dam. He had a
small star and snip on his face, and one
hind white sock.

Within half an hour the colt had
made several attempts to sort out his
long legs and stand up. On about the

fourth try, he managed to stand spraddle-legged for a short time before he collapsed in a heap, only to struggle and try again. I looked over at Liz, and saw that she just loved every minute of this. I knew too, that no matter how many times the miracle of birth would be observed, it would always be just that - a miracle.

Soon, the colt found the teats and nursed vigorously with his little dark tail swishing enthusiastically. Liz laid out the placenta to check that it was all there, and when the afterbirth had come away successfully, we cleaned up the stall and left mother and baby to their rest. There was no rest for us, however, as morning chores had been started and I, at least had to get to work.

After that, the foals began to arrive in quick succession. There were twenty-three in all, so there were many nights of interrupted sleep as we checked and watched the new babies arriving. When the foals were a few days old, we started halter breaking them to lead. It took two of us to take the mares and foals out each day; one to lead the mare, and one holding on to a rambunctious baby.

Once the foals were all on the ground the yearlings had to be readied for the Spring Sale. Halter broken as foals, weaned and turned out, they hadn't had much handling since. They were bratty and hard to manage at first, but soon settled down to being groomed and clipped and led about. Their feet were trimmed, and the colts were gelded – an operation we were all required to watch and assist with.

The young horses that we had been training under saddle were also being readied for the sale. Fulmer trained horses were known to fetch a good price. The students of Fulmer had a reputation to live up to, and we all worked extremely hard to get the horses under our care ready. Desert Fire was not going to the sale as Mark was seeking a private buyer for him. As long as Mark paid the board for the horse, Liz had no complaints about the gelding staying on. Since Monty was already gone, and the gray wasn't going anywhere soon, I helped the other three girls get their horses ready.

As we worked, I gradually let it be known that my dad was living in England. This aroused a lot of interested speculation, and surprise that I had been here for seven months now, and had not contacted him. Almost daily, Liz, Mark, or one of the girls would ask me if I had written to my dad yet. I always shook my head, 'no.' I just felt so awkward about contacting him. I didn't know what to say, or where to begin. Liz finally helped me over the hurdle. We were working on the books in the office one day, and she said casually, "Lindsey, I looked up your dad's phone number...and I hope you don't mind, but I called him."

"You what?" The color drained out of my face, as I looked into her gray eyes. "What did you say? What did he say?" The pencil was shaking in my hands.

Liz smiled at my discomfort. "Relax, would you? He sounded very nice. He was pretty shocked that you are here in England, and he's dying to see you."

"He is?" I asked softly. "Why? He left us ten years ago."

"I don't know all the reasons behind that, Lindsey. I think you should go and find out for yourself. You need to re-acquaint yourself with him and his family. You have grandparents here too, you know."

"I do?" I hadn't thought about them for years. I had never met them of course; they had just been old people in ancient photographs.

"Oh my God, Liz. What should I do?"

"As soon as those horses get on the lorry for the Spring Sale, you are going to get on the train and go spend a week with your dad. Things will slack off a little bit here then, and we can cover for you. You'll regret it the rest of your life if you don't go to see them. You know I'm right." Then Liz did something that really surprised me. She enfolded me in a big hug, and held me tight. She muttered softly into my hair, "Just go. I'll make the arrangements, if you like."

"Oh thank-you Liz. That would be wonderful," I said as tears rolled down my cheeks. I felt as if a great burden had been lifted.

CHAPTER TWENTY-THREE

We were becoming like family at Fulmer. Whenever anyone had a birthday, Mrs. Culvers was informed, and a gorgeous birthday cake would appear at the evening meal. On the night of April the fifteenth, it was my turn and when I came into the dining hall I was serenaded with Happy Birthday, and showered with gifts. My cake was chocolate, decorated with pink and blue sugar horses. My mom had phoned to wish me a happy birthday; she and Victoria were preparing to leave Estoril on the ship for the rest of the cruise through the Panama and on up the coast to Vancouver. She would be back home in May. I got cards and small gifts from my sisters, but no word from Russell.

Lying in bed later that night, I couldn't sleep. I was so mixed up about Mark and about Russell. We were so busy here; there had been no opportunities for Mark and me to slip away to Thornhylde. It was hard to maintain a student/pupil relationship with him. When I was near Mark, I wanted so much to hug and kiss him, and I knew from the smoldering looks he gave me, he felt the same. He was very strict about keeping a respectful distance from me, and I knew he did this not for his own reputation, for he could get a job anywhere with his qualifications, but for mine. I had to respect him for that, and go along with the ruse.

I had written to Russell faithfully, telling him about all the activities at Fulmer, but I had never received a reply. This nonsense had gone on long enough. I started to get angry. That night, I decided to go down to the phone in the hall, and talk to him in person. I knew it would be about seven in the morning there, and he should be just coming in from milking the cows.

I threw on some jeans and a sweater, slipped into my runners, and tiptoed down the stairs. All was in darkness. I turned on the hall light and placed the call.

Three rings, and then there was the voice I had not heard for nine long months. I gripped the receiver tightly. My palms were sweating.

"Hallo, Livingston's," he said.

"Hi Russell, it's Lindsey." There was silence on the line. "It's my birthday." No answer. "Russell, please talk to me," I pleaded. I could hear him breathing, it was so quiet, and then he said, "I can't. I...I'm sorry." And then he hung up.

I couldn't believe it! I heard the dial tone but it didn't occur to me to hang up until an automated voice come on the line and said, "Please hang up, your call has been disconnected."

Angry and shocked, I replaced the receiver. I switched off the light, and with my back to the wall, crumpled to the floor in the darkness. I laid my head on my knees and let the tears come while I cursed Russell and his callous stupidity. *Why didn't that jerk know that I still loved him?*

I didn't really have a plan or maybe I didn't even realize what I was doing, when I got up and slipped out the door into a heavy rain. I ducked my head down, and headed for Mark's cottage. My tears mingled with the rain, and I arrived at his door-soaking wet. I knocked gently.

The door opened a crack, as Mark appeared holding a blanket around his torso, and then his arm shot out as he grabbed me by the sweater and jerked me inside. "Jaysus Canada! What are you doing here? Did anybody see you come? Do you want to get us both run off the place?" He kicked the door shut. I had never seen him angry, and it scared me. I stood there, wet and sobbing as he regarded me quizzically.

"What's happened then?" he asked in a more gentle tone. When I didn't answer, he said with a jerk of his head, " Go on in there, and sit on the bed. I'll bring you a drink."

I went in and sat gingerly on the edge of the tousled bed. A soft light glowed from a small lamp on the beside table, which was littered with dressage and jumping horse magazines. In a moment Mark was back, handing me a glass half full of a dark amber liquid. I sniffed it suspiciously. "What is it?" I asked.

"It's brandy," Mark said as he lowered himself into a basket chair beside the small table. "Drink it up. It'll chase away your chills." He took a swig of his own brandy.

"Now, what's got you all in a tizzy at this hour of the night? Did one of the horses die?"

I took a deep breath, and tossed back the brandy, feeling it burn all the way to my toes. "No, I blubbered. It's Russell. He's the only one I didn't hear from for my birthday. I couldn't sleep, and I knew he'd be just coming in from the milking, so I went down and phoned him."

Mark drained his drink. "And...I suppose that did not go well, judging from the look of you?"

I nodded miserably, fresh tears falling down my cheeks. "He hung up on me."

Mark set his glass down on the table and muttered, "You don't deserve that, girl. I hope you told the bloody bastard to fek off!"

I managed a small grin through my tears at Mark's Irish expletive. "No," I

169

said. "I didn't get a chance to before he
hung up."
Mark stood up and came to me.
"Get those wet things off you and I'll
hang them by the heater. Get into bed
there, and warm yourself up."
I did as I was told. I was cold and
wet and I wasn't ready to go back yet.
The blanket fell from Mark's naked body
as he took my jeans and sweater to the
bathroom to hang up. In the dim
lamplight I couldn't help but admire his
wide, muscular shoulders, his narrow
waist and trim buttocks. Then he was
with me in the bed, pulling me into his
arms and comforting me with little kisses
while he smoothed my hair back. The
heat from his body and from the brandy
felt wonderful. I could feel warmth and
pleasure seeping into every part of my
body. I began to relax and respond to his
touch. He didn't hurry me. He had
learned patience by years of working with
high-strung hot-blooded horses, and no
doubt, inexperienced young women.
Later, when we lay with our legs
and fingers entwined, Mark said softly,
"Lindsey, have you thought about staying
here, in England?"
"Umm"...I moaned. I was almost
asleep. "No." I answered honestly,
starting to pay attention.
"Well, why not? You could get a
good position over here. Both Liz and I

170

will give you good references. You're a
good rider and trainer. You're a bit
hesitant with the teaching, but that will
come in time. The last semester here is
mostly on teaching lessons, so you'll gain
a lot more experience. And you have
family here. Your da's here."

"And *you're* here". I ventured to
add.

"Yes, I'm here. And I was
thinking...we could use some help at our
place."

"At Leamaneh?"

"Aye."

"I wouldn't want to put Paddy out
of a job."

"Oh, you wouldn't. There'll always
be a place for Paddy. But he's getting so
he can't train the young ones anymore.
That's why we've started sending them
out for training."

I was quiet for a moment, thinking
about working in that paradise, living in a
castle, riding and training those gorgeous
horses; going on the hunts... Then a
thought hit me. *Where did Mark fit in the
picture?*

"Oh yeah, right." I said. "And you'd
come home for Christmas with another
innocent young gal in tow, and I'd be so
jealous, I'd scratch your eyes out!"

He chuckled. "There you go, being
cynical again." He gave me a kiss. "I
wouldn't do that to you. And, just so you

know, you are the only girl I have ever brought home to Leamaneh."

"Really Mark? I find that hard to believe."

"Believe it," he said. "It's true."

"Well then," I said seriously. "I would need to know where we are going with this relationship."

Mark sighed deeply. "I don't know. I'm a bad boy. I've had lots of women, and I'm not sure if I can be faithful to just one. I might break your heart, and I would hate to do that. I like you an awful lot. It would be great if you would stay for another year, so we could see if it's going to work out. That is, if it's all over with Russell. You'd have to decide about that."

"I know. I'm so mixed up right now. I'm trying not to fall in love with you, but it's very difficult. You've been so good to me, and I love being with you. It's very tempting to stay on for a while. I actually hadn't thought of it. The thing is...I'm torn now between two countries and two men. I'd like to stay here with you, but I'd also like to go home and see if I can work it out with Russell. And then, my mom will be there in Canada, and my two sisters, and a lot of friends, and my horse, Redwing, and Buck the dog and Ying-Yang, my kitty..."

"Well, you don't have to decide tonight," Mark said. "And, if you don't get going, it will be daylight. You'd better skedaddle."

"You're right," I agreed, reluctantly pushing back the covers and recoiling against the cold air. "Augh! It's cold!" I made a dash for the bathroom and quickly put my clothes on. They were still slightly damp. Shivering, I went back into the bedroom for one last goodnight kiss. Mark held me tight.

"Take care, lass," he whispered. "Put that man out of your head and get some sleep. See you at breakfast."

" See you," I said, and I gave his hair a rumple. I opened the door slightly and seeing no movements anywhere, stepped out into what was left of the night. Thankfully, the rain had quit. I kept to the shadow of the bushes, moving slowly and went up to the big house, which was still in darkness. No one saw or heard me creep up the stairs to bed.

CHAPTER TWENTY-FOUR

True to her word, Liz made all the arrangements for my trip to Newcastle. The day after the horses were loaded up in the huge lorry and trucked to the auction, I found myself on the train heading for a meeting with my estranged father.

I was in much need of a rest, and was quite happy to just sit and relax, watching the beautiful English countryside flash by. 'Oh to be in England, now that spring is here...' I remembered reading that poem, even learning some of it, back in grade eight or nine. I just couldn't remember which of the English poets had penned those lines, but surely he had looked upon the same scenes that I was seeing. The greens of pasture, trees, and shrubs were so pure and vibrant – different again from Ireland – and it seemed that all the hedges were lined with purple or white lilacs, primroses, wild yellow broom, or honeysuckle.

I had planned to be polite, yet distant with my father. I was determined not to show any emotion about being reunited with him. I was going out of a sense of obligation and curiosity, not because I wanted to see him.

All that changed in an instant when I alighted from the train, and heard my name called immediately. "Lindsey! Over here!" I looked in the direction of the very British voice, and saw a tall man with gray hair standing on the other side of the station gate. He was dressed in a business suit and carried a newspaper and umbrella. *Typical Englishman*, I snorted with derision. The only thing missing was the bowler hat. I shouldered my backpack and moved in his direction. When I got closer, I was surprised to find myself looking into a mirror reflection of my own blue eyes. His smile, his teeth, and the squarish shape of his head – they were all mine! A strange sensation of shock and recognition pulsed through my body. He held out his arms, and I fell into them like a long lost puppy dog. I burst into tears, crying against the rough wool material of his greatcoat as he held me tight. "Why, Daddy, why?" I sobbed. "Why did you leave us? I never knew what happened."

My dad laid his cheek against mine and then held me away from him as he looked into my face. "Look what a lovely girl you've grown up to be. You're so beautiful!" He couldn't stop staring at me.

As gratifying as his praise was, I didn't want to hear this. I wanted answers.

"Dad, why didn't you keep in touch with us? Why didn't you write? Why didn't

you send us birthday cards or presents,
or anything at Christmas? Why did you
just disappear? I didn't even know you
lived over here until Mom told me, just
before I started at Fulmer. Why didn't you
tell me where you were? Why?"--

"Whoa! Hold it!" Dad said, laughter
making the corners of his deep blue eyes
crinkle. "So many questions! We have a
lot of catching up to do." He stepped
back and took my arm, eyeing my
backpack. "Is that all the luggage you
have?" he asked.

I nodded. "I travel light. I don't
really need anything other than my work
clothes. I do have a dress and shoes, if
we have to go out."

"Well, come along. The car is this
way. We can talk while we drive. Jenny will
have dinner waiting, so we'd better get
going."

"Jenny?" I asked. "Is she your wife?"
I wiped my teary eyes on a tissue, and
blew my nose. I hoped I didn't look too
awful.

"Yes," Dad answered, unlocking the
small blue car, and holding the door open
for me. I threw my pack into the back
seat and got in. Well, I knew he had re-
married, but I felt jittery at the prospects
of meeting 'the wife', the 'other woman,'
the one he left my mother and three girls
for.... I fell silent.

"Lindsey," Dad started, "First of all, I want to tell you how sorry I am that I didn't keep in touch with you girls. I know now...seeing you...that it was a bad mistake, but it seemed the best thing to do at the time. And after a while, it got harder and harder to re-establish contact, once it was broken. I thought you especially, being the youngest, would just forget about me. I always hoped your mom would re-marry and then you would have a daddy. I'm sorry that never happened."

"Yeah, me too." I sighed. "I really missed not having a daddy like all my friends. I used to tell them that you were a Secret Agent and you could only visit us at night because you had to travel incognito when you were in town on a mission. I think some of my friends actually believed it for a while." Dad looked over at me sympathetically. "Oh, that's sad, that a little girl had to make up a fantasy dad."

"Yeah, well... whatever...I guess it helped me cope." I was quiet for a bit, thinking how to phrase my next question. I just plunged in. "Dad, what happened in the marriage that you had to leave? I can see a relationship not working out, but how could you leave your children? I just can't understand it, and I guess I'm still mad and hurt about it."

Dad shrugged and looked sad. "I'm very sorry Lindsey. Affairs of the heart are difficult to understand. Sometimes we have to make choices, and those choices usually hurt one while they benefit another. I chose to return to my high school sweetheart and my heritage, and that choice has hurt you kids more than I realized at the time."

"Tell me more." I said. "I want to know everything."

"Okay," he said. "Put yourself in my shoes for a minute. Do you have a high school sweetheart?" I looked at him sideways. *What was he getting at?*

"Yes, actually I do, or I did until I left to come over here. He wasn't very happy about me leaving for a year."

"What's his name?"

"Russell Livingston. His folks have a dairy farm, and he's into rodeo. Calf roping is his specialty." I was going to tell Dad more about Russell, but he interrupted.

"Okay Lindsey, say you left your high school sweetheart to come over here to take a riding course for the year. Have you got a boyfriend over here?" *What could I say, oh yeah I'm having an affair with my riding instructor?* Instead, I just said, "I'm much too busy for that."

"Right. Just say you dated a fellow over here then, and he was handsome

and nice, and he wined and dined you
and got you pregnant."

I blushed hotly. *Where was he
going with this? Did he know about Mark?
How could he?*

"So," Dad continued, you decided to
get married. And you no sooner got the
baby weaned off your breast, when you
found out there was another bun in the
oven...and this went on until there were
three."

"Oh my God, Dad, weren't *any* of
us wanted?" I was shocked.

"No, no, don't get me wrong!
Nobody really *planned* a family in those
days. The kids just came along, and you
coped somehow. It wasn't that you
weren't loved or wanted; not at all."

"What then?" I asked.

"Well, to continue this hypothetical
scene, say that all this time you were
homesick for Canada and Russell. You
couldn't stop thinking about him, even
though you had a life here, and you
wanted with all your heart to go back
home to him. And then say he started
writing to you and you rekindled that old
flame, and you went for a visit, and found
you were crazy about him, and you just
decided to leave it all behind and stay."

"Even if it meant leaving my kids?" I
asked.

"Yes, even if it meant leaving your
kids. Get the picture?"

I certainly did. The parallels between his life and mine were too similar to be real. I now understood the dilemma he faced ten years ago.

"Dad, I understand now. You put your personal happiness ahead of the well being of your children. That was *your* choice. For me, if I couldn't have taken my kids with me, I would not have left. That would be *my* choice."

"Well," he said, "I knew you kids would be better off with your mother. And, I told you that choices have a way of helping one side and hurting the other."

"Maybe so, but it wouldn't have been so bad if you had kept in touch. Not hearing from you all those years was the hardest, and not ever being told why. It's done some damage, Dad."

"I'm trying to repair some of that damage right now, my darling." He reached over and took my hand and gave it a squeeze.

I turned and looked into his eyes. "Yes, you are Dad, and it's about time. You should write to Maryanne and Sarah too; they need to know the truth too."

"You're right, I will."

We were driving through a tract of unfenced land heavily wooded with beech and elm trees. Hedges and farms dotted the countryside and away in the distance, I could just see the blue/silver glint of the ocean. The road dipped suddenly and

180

wound over an arched bridge. "That's the River Alne," Dad said. "It winds around the north side of town and empties into the sea-estuary at Alnmouth on the Northumberland Heritage Coast. I'll take you to see Alnwick Castle. It's been the home of the Percy family since the 1300's. It's sometimes called the Windsor of the North. It's a magnificent castle." I could see that Dad was proud of the beautiful northern countryside and the great castle that had dominated the life and times of Alnwick for centuries.

"I stayed in a castle in Ireland at Christmas," I ventured. Dad looked surprised. "How did you end up in Ireland for Christmas? Why didn't you get in touch with us? We would have enjoyed having you here." There was a touch of reproach in his voice.

"I thought of it, but I was too shy to contact you, and I didn't want to upset your Christmas. I had a hard time even deciding if I wanted to see you at all. It's taken months of thought and talking it over with my friends, and Liz, the farm manager. She's really the one who made me see I *had* to come, even if *I* wasn't convinced."

Dad nodded. "I see. I think I understand. But if *we* had known you were here, we would have invited you. So...why did you go to Ireland, and what castle were you staying at?"

I thought for a second, wondering just how much to tell Dad. "Well, you see, I'm training a gray Thoroughbred gelding at Fulmer that belongs to the McTaggart family- "

The McTaggart Distillery family?" Dad's eyebrows shot up.

"Yes," I said. "Do you know them?"

"Well, not personally," Dad said, "but everyone knows of the whisky. The McTaggart's are a *very* well known and wealthy family in Great Britain." Dad was clearly interested in the rest of my story. "Go on," he said.

"Umm...well. Mark McTaggart is my riding instructor at Fulmer, and I had no idea who his family was or that he was well to do, but he invited me to come home with him for Christmas. He told me they had an extra bedroom and a few ponies we could ride. I just about fainted when we drove up to the castle, and I realized it was his home! And...oh Dad, you should see their stable! Everything is just top of the line and immaculate. They have a string of horses that would make the Queen jealous! It's a gorgeous place. I was just spoiled like a princess staying there, and I had a great time – all except for crossing the Irish Sea on the way back. I was so seasick; I didn't care if I died that day."

"Well, that's quite an adventure you had! Ah, this Mark must have been quite taken with you then, to ask you home for Christmas." It was more of a question than a statement.

"I think it was the horse connection," I lied. "I didn't know the colt belonged to them until they showed me his mother, and saddled her up for me to ride. The two are almost identical. I think they thought it was a good joke to see me try to figure out where I had seen her before. The Irish love to tease and jest. I think Mark's dad just wanted to meet the girl that was working on their prize colt. They have lots of household help, so it's no bother to have guests. They really treated me well. They're very down to earth, homey people. You wouldn't know they were filthy rich. I really like all of them very much." I didn't want to say how much I liked number three son, in particular.

We had arrived in the village of Seahouses. The cottages here were built of stone, and seemed to grow out from the hard rock on which they stood. Gaunt and strong, built to withstand the harsh weather and howling gales that pound the rugged coastline, they stood in a resolute line facing the sea. We pulled up in front of one of five identical white houses. "Your uncles live in those three," Dad said, with a jerk of his head. "They'll be over to meet you later. And your grandparents live in the end one."

"I didn't know I had uncles." I said. "Who are they?"

"Well, there's Tom, Dick and Harry. They're all fishermen. They bring in the kippers. I'm the only one that's in the Insurance Business." Dad was out of the car, and motioning for me to come in. "Come and meet the family."

"Tom, Dick and Harry?" I asked, incredulous, as I trudged up the stone walkway behind him. "Are you kidding me?"

Dad laughed. "No, I'm not. I guess my mother couldn't think of any more boy names when I came along, so they called me Cliff, after the famous cliffs above the harbor." He opened the front door and stood aside. A small woman of about fifty immediately met me and took my hand. She had a lovely soft face, blue eyes, and gray hair with smooth rosy cheeks, and a light shade of lipstick on her small mouth. "Lindsey!" she smiled a welcome. "It's *such* a pleasure to meet you." She was pretty and the dimples on the corners of her mouth made her look younger than she was. In spite of myself, I felt drawn to her and liked her immediately.

"Hello Jenny," I said, as warmly as I could. "It's great to be here."

I was brought into the warm and cozy sitting room where an elderly couple had been sitting by the open fireplace. "Here's your Gram and Gramps," Dad said. To his parents, he said, "Here she is, at long last!" My Gram was on the heavy side, with thick ankles but she had a ready smile and warm, strong arms, which enfolded me in a big hug. Gramps was a little more reserved, with bandy legs and a white moustache that tickled my cheek, as he hugged me and welcomed me to Seahouses.

As I looked over his shoulder, I could see a young boy sitting in a wide window-seat, set in the depth of the stone wall. Dad said, "I have a surprise for you, Lindsey." He motioned the lad over. The boy, whom I judged to be nine or ten, came over reluctantly, and stood in front of me, looking uncomfortable. Dad put his arm around the boy. "Percy, I would like you to meet Lindsey... say hello to your sister." The boy looked up at me shyly, and extended his hand. "Hello Lindsey," he said politely.

"My brother?" I stared at him for a split second, my eyes wide and I'm sure with my mouth hanging open. "Oh my God! I have a brother!" I ignored his offered hand, and pulled him into a tight embrace, while I tousled his blond hair. "I've always wanted a little brother!" I said with emotion.

After that, there was excited chatter as we sat down to a roast chicken dinner with all the trimmings and a gooseberry pie for dessert. Percy plied me with questions about Canada, about cowboys and Indians and horses, the pets I had at home and about his older sisters and his cousins. My dad said, "I think we'll have to plan a trip out to Canada to see it for yourselves. Now, we'll have a reason to go."

I spent a glorious week with my new family in the pretty and hospitable little fishing village. I tasted the famous kippers in some of the little café's and inns, and in my uncles' modest homes. Percy and I walked the beaches and climbed the cliffs, admiring the breathtaking scenery. I told him how I knew that he was named for the Percy family at Alnwick Castle who had inhabited the area since 1309. We toured the castle, marveling at the sheer size of it, the lavish Italian Resaissance style, the fabulous paintings by Canaletto, Titian and Van Dyke, the ornate ebony inlay cabinets, the exquisite porcelain, silver and many other antiquities.

At the end of my visit, I was lonesome for Mark and ready to get back to work with the horses. I was in love with, and torn by my feelings for two very different men and two beautiful countries.

CHAPTER TWENTY-FIVE

As soon as I got back to Fulmer, everyone questioned me about my visit with my dad and family. At supper that night Mark also asked how it went, and seemed pleased that I had made the journey and had resolved some issues with my dad. "Hey Canada," he said, flashing me that wide smile, "Guess who foaled while you were gone?"

"I don't know, who?" I asked, chewing thoughtfully. The mares had all been re-bred and turned out to summer pasture with their foals. We weren't expecting any more, as far as I knew. "Desert Wind! That's who! She had a black filly. My da says she's just a beauty. And he was wondering... if you'd like to name her, seeing you rode the mare and trained Desert Fire."

I gave Mark a knowing look. A mischievous smile was playing at the corners of my mouth. A name had already popped into my head. "Yes, I would...how about Desert Rose? The roses are really special at Leamaneh."

Mark actually blushed. "Aye," he said, returning the intimate look. "Desert Rose would be perfect. I'll tell me da." Thank-you for the lovely name."

"Well, thank your da from me for letting me name her. And if he doesn't like it, I'll think of something else."

"Oh, I'm sure he'll like it fine." Mark rose from the table and dropped a hand on my shoulder, giving it a squeeze as he went by.

The yearlings and young horses that we girls had started under saddle were sold. Now was the time of year that we concentrated on giving lessons on our school horses, and preparing our students and horses for the shows. All four of us were now competent in looking after almost any detail on the farm. We knew how to run the office, do the ordering for feed or vet supplies, doctor minor injuries, handle a mare or stallion for breeding, give a lesson, start a colt, or school a hunter over jumps. Liz and Joe took advantage of four full-time helpers, and went on a much-needed holiday to the Jersey Isles.

I hardly saw Mark and when he was around, there was no time to be alone. He was in demand for judging Pony Club events and since we didn't need much supervision now, he was free to compete on the show jumping circuit himself. He'd had Merlin shipped over from Ireland and was busy campaigning the big chestnut, as well as starting Desert Fire in some novice shows. I was painfully aware that many young women entered these competitions and that he probably didn't lack for female company while he was away. I missed him, and I entertained wild fantasies about him when he was gone but I steeled myself against the feeling; knowing that in all probability it was good that we were separated. The time was closing in fast when I would have to make a decision to stay in England or go home to Canada.

The summer was spent traveling around to as many small shows in the district as we could manage. For some of these, we took our horses by shank's pony, that is, riding one and leading two more tied head to tail by a short cotton rope. I liked to ride Chester as he had a good fast walk and he wasn't spooky or silly about traffic, dogs, or laundry flapping on the line. He was also a good, honest little jumper and great fun to compete on. He loved to gallop over steeplechase fences, and he was such a show-off when we were on parade. Plain as he was, he liked to think he was the center of attention, despite being outclassed by better-bred horses than he. Whenever he thought the occasion was right, he would strike out with a park walk – pointing his toes and then slapping his feet down with a snap. I won several rosettes with him, which I was careful not to leave anywhere near his pendulous lips. He was known to eat anything within reach that even resembled food.

I competed on Blackjack in a Novice competition at the Taunton Jumping Festival, and we won the event! He was much stronger now and more muscled since the Spring Training Event I had ridden him in at Fulmer. He was also much better behaved, although he still needed to gallop before settling down to work. A nice, controlled canter just didn't do it. He could shake the liver out of me if I didn't let him move out and really run. He was fit for the event, and even the up and down of the roads and tracks in the cross-country phase didn't slow him down. The springy turf helped him fly over the fences, and his galloping over the steeplechase gave us a very fast time. Even with his poor extended trot in the dressage, we came out on top with points and so won the Cup and a huge rosette for the day. His performance brought him to the attention of a Mr. Richard Stillwell. After speaking to me and congratulating me, he contacted Blackjack's owner and arranged to buy the temperamental black gelding. I was deeply disappointed that Mark hadn't been there to witness my success and share in my happiness.

Two of my students, Jill and Clarissa, were entered in the Grade C Jumping Competion that same day on Tinkerbelle and Mustard Sauce. The bay mare made her not so efficient rider look good - practically jumping the course herself. The pair took third place with a clear round but a slower time than the first two finishers. Clarissa was not so lucky, as Mustard Sauce put a foot down in the water jump, and finding no support, nearly fell unseating her rider. My plucky student was not hurt, but decided to withdraw from the competition.

When Mark returned to Fulmer with his two horses, he had already heard about my win on Blackjack at the Taunton Jumping Festival. Horse gossip travels from show to show with the competitors, grooms, and owners. All public and personal information is fodder for talk at the after parties or in the barns and pubs after the shows. Likewise, I had heard that he did well at the Badminton Horse Trials with Merlin, placing fourth in a tough international competition. It seemed we had some celebrating to do.

Mark found me in the barn, cleaning tack. I was alone at the moment, but the other girls were around somewhere, working at odd jobs. I heard the whistle of some Irish tune, and recognized the jaunty stride of his boots upon the cobblestones. He looked in the door of the tack room, a huge smile lighting up his face.

"Hi Canada! There you are!" Then, glancing quickly around to make sure no-one was looking, he slid his arms around me and pulled me against him, kissing me hard. "Oh God, I've missed you, " he breathed into my hair.

I flushed deeply, excited by his touch, and longing to release my pent up emotion. I was thrilled to see him. "Careful...the girls are about," I cautioned. He let me go, reluctantly.

"Come for a drink with me tonight, will you? At the pub?" We can toast each other's victories. I want to hear about the show, and tell you about Badminton."

"I'd love to Mark," I said with a smile. "But I think you should ask the other girls to come too. We've all had various successes thanks to your expert instruction, and I think they'd love a chance to talk to you about teaching opportunities and what the prospects are out there for us students."

Mark looked clearly disappointed, and I was somewhat gratified that he wanted to visit with me alone. He crossed his arms and regarded me evenly, as I continued to polish the saddle I had been working on. "Is this a rebuff for leaving you alone so long?" he asked gently.

"No, not exactly. I...I want to be with you too, maybe too much. But I think it will be too obvious that there's something going on between us if we go out together tonight. They're not completely stupid, and they *are* my best friends."

Mark grinned then. "Okay, I'll go and find them and ask them *all* out. I guess I'm a lucky devil if *four* beautiful young women want to go out with me."

"I'd say you're a lucky devil anyway", and I threw a brush at him. He ducked, and went out whistling that damned Irish tune.

CHAPTER TWENTY-SIX

We had just sat down to our evening meal the next night, when Joe came in and dropped two letters by my plate. "Letters from home, Lindsey," he announced. I looked at the envelopes quickly, recognizing Mom's handwriting, and on the one underneath – Russell's! Eleven months without a word, and now when I least expected it, here was the long awaited letter! I must have looked like I'd just seen a ghost. Everyone was staring at me, including Mark. I think he knew what I held in my hand.

I stood up and pushed my chair back. "Excuse me...I'm not hungry," I muttered. I didn't' dare look at Mark as I turned and left the dining room clutching my letters to my breast. I bounded up the stairs to my room and threw myself on my bed, breathing hard. I turned Russell's letter over and over in my hands, holding it to my face, seeing him so clearly in my mind as I tried to summon the courage to open it. My hands were shaking. I forced myself to calm down and opened Mom's letter first.

She was back home after a wonderful trip through the Panama Canal and up the west coast of the U.S. She and Victoria had enjoyed sightseeing in San Diego and Los Angeles. She told me that Buckwheat and Ying Yang were fine, and

that she had talked to Pam about
Redwing and things were also good there.
Victoria was back in the nursing home
with enough pictures and adventures to
talk about for a whole year. Since the
rental lease wasn't up on our farm until
the end of August, Mom had rented an
apartment in a newer subdivision in
Abbotsford. A couple of times in the
letter, she mentioned a man named Paul
Hanson, a widower that she had met on
board, and I wondered if there might be a
romance blossoming. Hmm...interesting.
     Finally I could wait no longer.
Supper would be over if I didn't hurry up,
and the girls would be coming upstairs to
see what my news was. I closed my eyes,
said a quick prayer to the Almighty, and
slit Russell's letter open.
     Dear Lindsey,
     I don't know where to begin. There
is so much to be said; so much that is
better left unsaid. Last week Mom was
putting socks and underwear away in my
top drawer and she found all your letters
that I had stashed in there – unopened.
She took them out to my dad, and he
confronted me with the letters and made
me promise to read them and give you
some kind of a response. He told me in no
uncertain terms that I was being a jerk
and that you were some kind of saint for
putting up with my silence for so long. He

*made me promise to write to you, even if
it was a "get lost" letter.
Well I can't do that to you. I love
you. Always have, always will. I know I
have a weird way of showing that love. I
thought if I could possess you, you would
stay, but I know now that I only drove you
away with my selfishness. I've grown up
some since then.
I read all of your wonderful letters, over
and over again and I cried like a baby.
Nowhere, in any of them, is there any
blame or reproach for the way I treated
you
         I see in your last letter, you have
re-united with your dad, and that you
have a brother you didn't know about. I
can understand your quandary about
staying in England for a year or two to
work. It's got to be hard to be torn
between two families and countries.
Whatever you decide, I'll be here for you,
as a friend or more if you want.*

All my love,

Russell

I read the letter three times. Then I
slipped it under my pillow, turned on my
belly, and let the tears of relief come. I
must have dozed off after a little while,
because all of a sudden I smelled
something delicious, and Joan was sitting

on the end of my bed. "I brought you up some supper," she said. "I knew you'd be hungry." Her dark eyes met my tear – stained blues as I sat up and took the offered plate.

"Thanks pal," I smiled at her. "You're a life-saver." I dug my fork into the tender pastry covering a chicken and vegetable stew. I was starving.

"So!" Joan said. "What's up? Does he love you or love you not?" Joan, Donnie and Britt-Marie were well aware of my problems with Russell. That part of my life was not secret from them; only out of necessity my affair with Mark was. I reached under my pillow and tossed her the letter, which she grabbed and read almost greedily. Her face lit up with glee as she whooped and grabbed me around the neck, almost spilling my dinner into the bedclothes. "Yay! He loves you! You're going home!" she yelled.

Donalda and Britt-Marie came into the room. "What's the news?" Donnie asked. "We're all dying of curiosity!"

Joan passed them my letter and after they both read it, there was lots of excited chatter. They were all genuinely happy for me that I had finally heard from my 'Canadian cowboy'.

Joan turned serious. "Mark was very quiet at dinner. He seemed upset. Uh...is there something going on between you two?" I looked up, surprised.

"No. Why? We're good friends. We had to talk about something on our long trip to Ireland. I've told him about Russell."

Joan curled up on my bed and wrapped her arms around her knees. "I think he's worried that you're going back to Canada. I think he's hoping you'll stay here."

"I've been considering it," I said. Then, to change the subject, I asked her, "What are you going to do? We've only got six weeks left together, and then we'll all be going our separate ways." This led to a general discussion about where we would find jobs once we got our certificates. I was thankful to have the conversation steer away from my relationship with Mark. I didn't want to have to confront my feelings for him right now.

I had been looking for an opportunity to talk to Mark, but it didn't come until three days later when he rode into the yard on Desert Fire. He had been out with the local hunt club on a 'puppy walk.' These were training rides for young horses and outings for the young hounds to learn the basics of following a scent. Britt-Marie had gone into Taunton for her day off. Donnie was running the office, and Joan was teaching a lesson in the covered arena.

I had been out to check on the mares and foals, and noticed that Velvet Breeze's little colt had a cut on a hind leg. I could have got Joan to help with the colt later, but it was a good excuse to get Mark alone, and I used it.

"Mark," I called, when he came into the barn leading the gray. "There's nobody around, and I need help to get one of the colts into the barn to treat a cut. Could you give me a hand when you've looked after Desert Fire?"

"Sure thing, Canada. Be right with you." He went off whistling, looking pleased, while I went to fetch a halter for the mare. He met me out in the mare paddock and we led Velvet Breeze and her fuzzy chestnut colt into a large stall in the barn. Mark looked at the cut, and commended me for noticing it. "These small cuts can get infected quickly. See... already his fetlock is swelling. He'll need a shot of penicillin."

It was a nice feeling, working side by side with Mark on the little colt. I cleaned the wound with disinfectant, bandaged his leg, and gave him his needle. Mark let me do everything. He just held the colt still for me. I was kneeling in the straw beside the colt's leg as I finished taping the bandage. I put the supplies back into the vet kit. Mark let the colt go and dropped to his knees beside me. His arm slid around my waist and gently he pushed me down into the soft straw. His face was suddenly over mine and he was kissing me. I held him close and kissed him back. It was the only time we'd let ourselves get carried away; except maybe the night I went to his cottage. With the mare and foal watching curiously, we made sweet, passionate, desperate, love.

As we re-arranged our clothing Mark asked me, "What was in the letter then? What aren't you telling me?" I looked over at him and grinned. "I was just going to tell you, when you pushed me over and ravished my body. Is there straw in my hair?"

"Come here, and let's have a look." Mark turned me around and picked several wisps out of my pony- tail. He leaned against the side of the stall and pulled me against him. "You're leaving me, aren't you?" he said. "Does the Cowboy want you back?"

I laid my head against Mark's wide chest. I was suddenly overcome with emotion and found it hard to speak. I raised my head and looked into his intense blue eyes. "Yes, he wants me back...and it's going to be very hard to leave you...but I'm going." And then I added softly, "Is it possible to love two guys at the same time?"

Mark heaved a sigh. "Aye, lass. It's entirely possible... and impossible. I understand your feelings. I'm very fond of you too. I didn't want this to end. I was hoping you would stay, but I'm happy for you." He kissed me again, and then he said, "We'd better get out of here before we're missed." Reluctantly, we let go of each other and went back to work. I wished him luck for his next series of shows; the Royal at Nottingham, a Three Day Event at Leicester, and the Great Yorkshire Show. He was leaving in the morning and he had much to do to get ready.

CHAPTER TWENTY-SEVEN

All too soon, the summer and our year at Fulmer School of Equitation were over. The four of us who had started as Working Pupils and strangers from different countries had become the best of friends – no; more than friends – we were family.

As Liz handed out our British Horse Society certificates with hugs and tears she told us, "Life is full of beginnings and goodbyes...I hope you will all keep in touch and let us know how your careers are going. Joan, best of luck in Scotland. I understand you'll be managing your uncle's pony trekking business in Inverness. Donnie, it's been a pleasure working with you. You are taking many new skills back to New Zealand. I know you'll do very well in the horse business. Britt-Marie Larsgaard. Congratulations on landing a job in America! There are probably more horses in Kentucky than there are in all of England. It's a place I'd like to visit myself one day. Please keep in touch. And Canada...Lindsey, it's been wonderful getting to know you. I hear that romance is in the air for you back home, and that a job is waiting for you as well. Come back and visit your second home."

Then Mark stepped up and gave us

all hugs and a kiss on the cheek as he congratulated us on our year's work. For once I didn't have to hide the fact that I was going to miss him. We were all crying.

A few days before we were all to vacate Bredalbane House to make room for the next four students that would soon be arriving, Mark arrived at the farm from his jumping competitions. We all flocked around the horse -box and helped him unload Desert Fire and Merlin, plying him with questions about his performances.

"Well," he grinned, "It wasn't all bad. The ground was very hard at the Royal, and neither horse could stand jarring on the legs. They didn't like the footing, so we were unsuccessful. That's the way it goes sometimes."

I took hold of Desert Fire's lead rope and gave the gelding an affectionate neck rub. "You tried your best though, didn't you, little sweetie?" I crooned to him.

"Yes, he did well, Canada. You've done a great job starting him. He's willing and confident and easy to handle. He can't do the big jumps yet, but then I don't expect him too either. He's still young."

Britt-Marie and Joan were helping to unload the horses and tack as well. Britt said, "So...did you win anything? We expect our teacher to come home with *some* trophies."

"Of course I wouldn't want to disappoint my little protégés." Mark said, laughing. He tweaked one of her braids playfully. "At Leicester, Merlin won the Gambler's Stakes over pretty big fences, and...get this...at Yorkshire, he won a first in each of his classes, including the Championship." Mark was grinning from ear to ear as he backed the big chestnut out of the van. Joan flung herself at him, giving him a warm hug, which he returned. "Congratulations!" she beamed. I felt a little bit jealous, seeing her hug Mark.

"Well! That's more like it!" Britt-Marie grinned, as she carried Mark's saddle and bridles to the barn. I followed, leading Desert Fire.

"Way to go, Irish!" I said. I didn't trust myself to touch him in front of the other girls. He turned and gave me a wink, which said many things – he accepted my praise, he was happy to see me, and he understood why I didn't hug him.

We had so little time left. Liz was going to drive us to the train station where she had picked us all up, almost a year ago. Joan was heading straight up to Inverness; Britt-Marie was going home to Stockholm to see her family before flying to Kentucky to start her new job at a racing stable, Donnie was flying home to New Zealand, and my flight was booked from London's Heathrow Airport to Vancouver, B.C. I had telephoned my mom to tell her my arrival time. She said someone would be there to meet me, but she wasn't sure which family member it would be. They were all looking forward to having me home. I was getting excited too!

Mark came out to the arena the next morning to watch me teach my last lesson with Clarissa. She was riding Mustard Sauce. I was no longer nervous when Mark watched me work. I was confident in what I was doing, and knew what I wanted to accomplish with horse and rider. I called out to her, "Squeeze those reins like a sponge, Clarissa; don't pull. Keep your leg on, and push her up into the bit with your seat. That's it. Now...just practice those serpentines for a couple of minutes while I talk to Mr. McTaggart."

"Mr. McTaggart, is it?" he grinned, as I approached.

"Mr. McTaggart," I said, slapping my riding crop against my leather boots, just the way he did with us in lessons. "Would you be wanting something, or did you just come to bother me when I'm trying to work?" I put on my best Irish accent.

His grin was infectious. "Actually I
do want something. I was wondering if
you would like to spend a day with me at
Thornhylde before you go?"

My shock must have registered on
my face. "Oh God, Mark! I can't!
My flight is booked for tomorrow
afternoon. I can't change it now. Why
didn't you ask me sooner? We could have
made a plan. I would have loved to go
with you to Thornhylde one last time. I
never did get to explore the place."

He was still grinning at me. "Would
you be quiet girl, and let me tell you
something?"

"Okay...what?" He took my hand
through the bars of the arena and played
with my fingers. I shot a nervous glance
to the left and right, but saw no one.
Clarissa was diligently practicing her
serpentines. "Mark...don't." I tried to pull
my hand away.

"What would you say," he said
seriously now," If your flight had been
delayed a day, and someone had paid the
difference on the fare, just so he could
spend a day with you?"

My jaw dropped and my eyes
opened wide. "Mark! You didn't!" Then,
seeing the twinkle in his eyes, I said, "Did
you?"

"Aye, I did," he said softly. I
swallowed hard. Tears sprung to my eyes.
I pulled my hand away.

"Jaysus!" I didn't know what else to say. He threw his head back and laughed out loud. Then I thought of something else.

"But Mark, Liz is taking us to the train tomorrow morning. We're all going to London together. How am I going to get out of that?"

"Easy," he said. "You say your goodbyes and you get on the train, but you get off at Wellington. I'll be there to meet you."

"But that's only one stop away. What will I tell the girls?" He shook his head at me, and caught his lower lip in his teeth.

"How about the truth? What does it matter now? You'll have twenty minutes to explain to them what's been under their noses for the past eight months."

"Oh my God, Mark! They'll have an absolute fit!" I was starting to grin now too, thinking of the reaction I would get.

"Will you do it, Canada? Will you get off at Wellington?"

" I will." I said, serious again. "If you're sure you've changed my flight and all."

"I have...and you'll have to phone your mam again tonight to let her know you'll be arriving Saturday morning, not Friday as planned."

"Right. Now, how do you expect me to finish this lesson? You've gone and

fuzzed me up and got me all excited –you
Irish Devil, you!"
Mark smiled and turned to go.
"That's why you have a lesson plan, right?
Just follow the dots...see you tomorrow."

CHAPTER TWENTY-EIGHT

By eight a.m. the next morning, we had said our goodbyes to Mrs. Culvers, and Jeremy, her kitchen helper, and to Joe. Mark was nowhere to be seen. The horses had all been turned out for the day, and we didn't have to do any stalls. We were all fairly quiet as we drove away from Fulmer for the last time. All of us would have many memories of the people, horses, and life changing events that had occurred over the past year.

It was very hard to say goodbye to Liz. She had been our teacher, mother, friend and mentor over the past year. We would all miss her. We were all bawling by the time we were on board and the train pulled out of the station.

We got a compartment to ourselves, and as soon as we were out of Taunton Station, I pulled myself together and said, "Girls, I have something to tell you."

"What?" they all chorused. Tissues came out and tears were mopped up. All eyes were upon me. I think they all thought that it was something about Russell – maybe that he had proposed to me, or something like that.

"I'm getting off at the next station. I'm not going to London today."

"What do you mean?" Joan asked. "What about your flight home? Have you changed your mind?" The other two girls echoed her questions.

"No, I'm meeting Mark and we're going to spend the day *and* night together at very private house he owns out by the old Abbey ruins. He's going to take me to the airport tomorrow." I watched and waited as the shock and disbelief set in and registered.

Joan's dark brown eyes sparkled with mischief. She jumped up and grabbed me in a bear hug. "I knew it!" she said. "I *thought* there was something between you two! Didn't I say so?"

Britt chimed in, "Well I must say, you hid it well. You lucky Canuck, you! He is *so* cute! He's so athletic and charming with that Irish accent." Donnie had blushed a deep shade of scarlet. She wasn't quite as outgoing and lenient in her views. She was genuinely embarrassed.

"But, Lindsey," she said in a quiet voice. "Aren't you going home to marry Russell? How could you do this?"

"I know it's hard to understand, Kiwi. But I love Mark in many ways too. It's going to be very hard to leave him. I seriously considered taking a job in England so I could be near him, but it probably wouldn't work for us. He's not ready to settle down, and when he does, his parents would want him to marry a good Irish 'catlick.'" I imitated Mark's accent as I said this. "We've become good friends, and more, but as you can imagine, we haven't had much time together. We've had to be very discreet. We just want to spend a last day together. I don't know if I'll ever see him again."

Joan said, "I thought something was going on that night when you disappeared at midnight, and didn't come back for a couple of hours. Were you with him?"

"Yeah...gee, I thought you were asleep. I went down to use the phone to call Russell. Remember, it was my birthday? He was the only one I hadn't heard from. He hung up on me, and I was so devastated I ran right to Mark's place, and of course he took me in." I smiled sheepishly.

"Right," Britt-Marie said. "And then there was the time he took you out for supper; he was so concerned that you had come off of Blackjack...and the trip to Ireland to his home. Oh yeah, it all adds up now. He was sweet on you right from the first."

In a few minutes, Wellington Station was announced. The train slowed but my heart was thumping fast. *Would Mark really be there?* I would look like an awful fool if he weren't. I hugged each of the girls in a tight embrace, tears threatening to fall again. "Goodbye...I love you guys," I whispered. I wiggled into the straps of my heavy backpack and picked up the duffel bag that contained my riding helmet and boots. "Life's an adventure, eh? See ya!"

They still looked shocked and stricken as I moved out into the corridor and then stood in the cubicle between the cars, waiting for the train to stop.

As soon as I alighted, I saw Mark coming towards me. Relief surged through me. He took my duffel bag with one hand and put his arm around me with the other, pulling me close for a kiss. We stood waving and grinning at the three faces pressed to the windows until the whistle blew, the steps were put up, and the train chugged out of our lives.

Mark was over six feet tall, and he had to look down at me. "I wasn't sure you'd get off, Canada." He smiled at me.

"I wasn't sure you'd be here," I grinned back. "There were some tense moments." We turned and headed for the Porsche. He flung my bags into the boot, and slid into the driver's seat.

"How did the girls react?" he asked. I filled him in on everything they said and did as we drove through the picturesque Somerset countryside.

At Thornhylde, I could see that Mark had been doing some improvements. The broken stone wall had been repaired, and the overgrown hedges and gardens had been trimmed and tidied. The place looked much neater and more attractive than I remembered it.

We entered by the red door. I waited in the kitchen while Mark took my bag up to the bedroom. "Everyone was wondering where you were this morning. They wanted to say goodbye to you," I told him when he came bouncing down the wide stairs.

"Well, I was here, getting things ready for you. I did some grocery shopping, chopped lots of wood for the fires, put flowers in every room, scrubbed the floors, waxed and polished the furniture, and washed all the bedding, trimmed the hedges, and mowed the lawns."

"You didn't do all that by yourself!" I chastised him. "I'll bet you didn't do the half of it. You're teasing me." I gave him a playful punch on the shoulder.

"Okay, so I had a little help. I hired a couple of women from the village to clean up." When I gave him a searching look, he added, "Oh they were fat and ugly – don't you give me that look!" He put his arms around me and pulled me against his chest. "They couldn't hold a candle to you, my little Canada." We shared a couple of kisses, and then Mark asked, "Would you like to go explore the grounds and have a picnic down by the stream?"

"My thoughts exactly. I'd love to!"

"Okay..."he said, releasing me. Grab that canvas bag over there by the door and we'll pack a few things". Mark yanked open the refrigerator door and took out a chunk of local cheese, fresh-baked bread, and a bottle of wine. He threw in some apples and chocolate. "How's that?" he asked.

"Perfect picnic fare." I laughed. "Let's go." Mark picked up a blanket that was draped across an easy chair in the corner, and together we stepped out into the sunshine. The hedges of box, holly, and ferns were alive with the twittering of many birds. It reminded me of my lilac hedge at home and the little sparrows that inhabited the tangle of branches. My thoughts drifted to my animals, my farm; my own place. The thing is, I could see myself living here just as easily. It was a strange feeling. Mark sensed my pensiveness, and asked, "What's on your mind?"

"Oh...I was just thinking how beautiful everything is, and comparing it in my mind to my own place. I stopped. "What's that birdcall? Sh...listen...that one."

"That's a Nightengale," Mark explained. "Do you not have those?"

I don't think so. I've heard of them, but never heard one. That's a beautiful song. I love listening to it. We walked hand in hand down the flag-stone path to

the bank of a river that formed
Thornhylde's southern boundary. The
property was open to this river, but was
otherwise completely enclosed by high
hedges of thorn, with deep woods of oak
and yew behind. There was a grove of
fruit trees, planted symmetrically
opposite the vegetable garden. I could
just see the reds and golds of ripe fruit
hanging on the trees. Then I was looking
at the sparkling light on the river; a flash
of blue – a Kingfisher; a shoal of black
streaks – tadpoles.

Mark set down the bag and spread
out the blanket. We took off our shoes
and socks and wriggled our feet in the
grass and lay back on our elbows, raising
our faces to the sun. Mark opened the
wine. He took a swig from the bottle,
wiped his mouth and passed it to me.
"Have some Madeira, ma dear-a?"

I tipped the bottle to my lips,
tasting the sweet, fruity flavor, nodding
with approval as I handed it back. "That's
good." Mark was looking at me intently. I
knew what he wanted. I leaned close and
kissed him, and felt his fingers starting to
undo my shirt.

We made love there on the
riverbank with the birds trilling and the
sun shining and a little breeze making
the boughs on the trees bounce.
Afterwards, Mark pulled me into the river
to cool off and wash. It was cold, but it

felt good. As we dried off in the sun on the blanket, we tore off chunks of bread and ate it with the cheese, washing it down with more wine. The Queen herself couldn't have enjoyed a finer feast.

Later in the afternoon back at the house, after we had explored all the rooms, Mark taught me to play Backgammon. We cooked dinner together, and I was surprised that he even knew how to put a meal together. "You know," I teased, "For a rich kid that's always had a nanny and kitchen maids, you're pretty capable at looking after yourself."

"Thanks," he said, wielding a knife on some vegetables like it was a sword, "I've been out on my own since I was sixteen, so I've had to learn a thing or two about survival."

I came up behind him and put my arms around his middle. "You've learned a thing or two, all right. And...you've taught me a thing or two as well. I guess I should thank you for that." He laid the knife down and turned to me. He looked into my eyes and smoothed my hair back before his kissed me long and deep. "Ah, Canada...you've been a pleasure to teach – both in the saddle and in the sack." We both laughed and exchanged easy banter as we prepared and later enjoyed grilled salmon with dill sauce, mixed salad greens, small whole new potatoes rolled

in butter and parsley, and more of that
delicious bakery bread.

We didn't sleep much. I never wanted the
night to end. I cried, knowing that this
would be the last time I could be with
Mark. He was tender and loving and
sweet, and I knew he was sad too. I kept
thinking of those lines from Joni
Mitchell's song about her lover trying
hard to please, and putting her at ease,
and loving her so naughty it made her
weak in the knees. That was us exactly.
Canadian and foreign; loving and leaving.
Why was it wrong for us to be together? I
wanted so much to just tell Mark that I
loved him, and would stay with him, and
yet, I was irresistibly pulled in the
direction of home. Mark wouldn't commit
to saying he loved me, as long as there
was the chance that I was going to renew
my romance with Russell. He wasn't
going to play 'second fiddle' to any other
man. I could understand his side of it
too. We talked about it half the night.
Even though it was hard to say goodbye,
we both felt that I should go home to
Canada; to Russell; that we should both
return to the lives we grew up with. Mark
said that if I wanted to come back, I was
to just let him know, and he would gladly
pay my fare.

In the morning, we closed up Thornhylde, got into the shiny red Porsche and made the drive to London's Heathrow Airport. We didn't talk much. There was nothing more to say. As I clung to him in one last embrace, Mark whispered against my cheek, "If you marry that cowboy, I want an invite to your wedding. Promise?"

Through my tears, I promised. I walked through the gates and didn't look back.

CHAPTER TWENTY-NINE

The last person I expected to see at the airport was Russell. As I stood on the down escalator that went to the baggage pickup, I was looking for Mom or my sister Maryanne. Then I saw the hat – the old, beat-up leather Australian cowboy hat, and underneath it, there was Russell standing stoic and solid. I didn't see anyone else I knew, so I walked purposely towards him and when we got close, we both opened our arms and melted into a great big long hug. He told me I looked good, and I told him he looked good too. Then we waited for my duffel and backpack to arrive on the conveyer belt. Russell scooped them both up, and we went out into the Vancouver sunshine (not liquid for a change) to his truck.

"How's the old beater running?" I asked.

"Just great," he smiled. "I keep her tuned up," he said as he swung my bags into the back and opened the door for me. I tossed my shoulder bag into the seat and climbed in.

Russell got in his side and put the key in the ignition. He was about to start the truck, but instead, he looked over at me and said, "You've been gone for a whole year, and you're going to sit away over there by the door?"

I laughed, picked up my shoulder bag and put in where I had been sitting, as I slid over closer to Russell. "There. How's that?" I grinned.

His deep blue eyes were on mine, as he said, "That's better." Then he put his right arm around my shoulders and held my hand with the other. "Lindsey," he said, "I only want to say this once, and then I want to forget it." I waited, serious now. He was having a hard time putting his thoughts into words, although I 'm sure he had rehearsed them many times already. "That night...before you left...I want to apologize for the way I treated you. I'm sorry I caused you so much heartache. I want to thank you for whacking me on the head, and I want you to know, I will never touch you again in that way." His fingers played with the ends of my hair, and his thumb stroked my cheek gently. Our eyes held each other for an instant, and then we were kissing just like old times. He felt so good to hold and kiss; I wondered how I could go from the arms of one man to another so easily. *Did I truly love them both, or did I just love the one I was with?*

Russell released me and started the truck. "We're going over to your sister's place," he told me. "All the family is there to welcome you back." He continued to hold my hand as he drove. As much as I wanted to see everyone, I felt giddy with tiredness. I had not slept much on my last night with Mark, and I had just lost eight hours on the flight. My inner clock was all mixed up with the time change and emotional turmoil I was in. I just wanted to sleep.

I said, "Russell, can we pick Redwing up from the arena tomorrow and go for a ride? I'm dying to see her."

Russell gave me a sideways glance. "Actually, Red's out at our place. She's up on the mountain pasture."

"Why?" I asked, suddenly. "Pam didn't say anything about that. "Why do you have her? She's supposed to be earning her keep as a lesson horse."

"Well, Pam thought she needed a break from training, so she asked your mom to take her out, and your mom asked me to look after her until you got home. Pam just thought that Red would be happier out on pasture instead of staying in a small paddock."

"Oh," I said. Something seemed a little fishy, but I was too tired to question it further. "Well, thanks for taking her. But I'm disappointed. I wanted to see her and go riding tomorrow."

"Oh we still can." Russell gave me a reassuring smile." I've got a mare at my place I'm keeping for someone. You can ride her up to the mountain and lead Red home. Or you can double with me on Sunny."

"No," that's too hard a climb for a horse to carry double. I'll ride your mare. Whose horse is it?"

"Oh, I'm just keeping her for a little while for a girl I know. She's a nice horse, a bay Anglo-Arab."

"Oh yeah?" I said, interested. "I had a bay Anglo-Arab at Fulmer. She's a sweetheart. She's beautiful and she can jump like a deer. Her name is Tinkerbelle. What's this mare's name?"

"She's registered as a half-Arab as My Flaire Lady. The girl that owned her called her Figgy."

"That's cute," I said. "What do you mean, the girl that *owned* her? Did you buy this horse?" Russell looked embarrassed. He squirmed a little in his seat.

"Well, yes…kind of," he hedged. "She belonged to a teenager who thought that boys were more interesting than horses. I thought I'd just ride the mare a bit and tune her up, and then re-sell her. She's a good horse, just going to waste.

"I see," I nodded. I was getting so sleepy I couldn't keep my eyes open any longer, and the mare's background was no longer interesting. I leaned on Russell's shoulder and dozed off until we got to Maryanne's house.

It was wonderful seeing all my family again. Jessie and Luke had grown and

changed so much in a year. I had small
gifts for everyone – souvenirs from
England, so it was kind of like Christmas.
As much as I enjoyed seeing everyone,
and telling them all about my year in
England, I couldn't wait to get home to
our little farm to see Buckwheat and Ying-
Yang. On the drive out to the valley, Mom
told me she had moved back into our
house at the end of August, and reported
that the Robson's had looked after the
animals and property very well. They had
left it clean and tidy.

I was curious about Redwing. I
asked," Why didn't Pam just bring her
over to our own place?"

Mom said, " Well, Russell offered to
look after her so that she could have the
company of another horse." And then
Mom changed the subject and diverted
my questions with one of her own.

"How did you get along with your
father?"

"Really good, actually." I said. "I set
myself up for not liking him, but when I
saw him, I just folded. We had a good talk
about your breakup, and I think I can
understand his side of it now. Hey Mom,
did you know I have a brother? And
grandparents? And uncles? I have a whole
bunch of family I knew nothing about.
And Jenny's really nice. I liked her right
away."

Mom said, "I'm glad you made the effort to go and get reacquainted. And yes, I did know about Percy. I just kept everything from you until you were old enough to understand things."

"Yeah, well, I'm not sure it was the right thing to do. You should have told us everything when we were little; then we wouldn't have had this big empty space in our lives where our dad should have been. Even Dad agreed that he should have kept in touch with all of us. He realizes it was a mistake, and he's sorry. I think he'd like to come over for a visit and make it up to Maryanne and Sarah."

Mom sighed. "As a single parent, I think I was just trying to shelter you girls from the truth because it was so painful. Its not easy being left for another woman."

"I know Mom, but we grew up thinking because he didn't love you, he didn't love us either. And once I met him, I knew that wasn't true. He does care about his girls. And I hope, if they come over, you'll be all right with that." I gave her an imploring look.

"Yes, that would be okay. I'm well over it now. There's been a lot of water under the bridge. It would be nice to have them come for a visit."
I felt good about that. I dozed off again, trying to catch up on my missed sleep.

Soon we were home with Buckwheat putting on a wild show of ecstatic greetings – he barked, raced around in circles of joy with one of his toys, came up to me repeatedly with a half jump and just about wagged his tail right off his back end. He had to come in the house and follow me everywhere. My kitty was a lot more restrained and dignified in her greeting. She allowed me to pick her up and hold her in my arms like a baby while she purred contentedly. It didn't last long. She wanted down, but she rubbed her body against my legs as I walked around. Both animals piled on my bed with me that night as I retired early, tired but happy to be home.

CHAPTER THIRTY

Russell was at my place by mid-morning riding Sunny and leading the bay mare. Red's halter was tied on to his saddle horn. I put my own saddle and bridle on Figgy, and mounted up. She seemed like a decent horse; nice rich deep bay color with a pretty star and snip on her face. Riding up to the mountain with Russell felt so good; everything was new and fresh to me. The country seemed so open and big after the small towns, narrow roads, and cobblestones that dominated the English countryside.

When we approached the meadow, Sundance threw his head up and blasted out a whinny. Redwing answered his call immediately. She came on the gallop, zigzagging through the trees like a barrel horse at the Calgary Stampede. She ploughed to a stop in front of Sunny, nickering and pawing. Then she sniffed Figgy, squealed and turned to kick. I turned the mare away just in time to miss a flying back hoof. I jumped off the bay, and gave Russell the reins to hold.

"Holy Cow, Russell! Is she ever fat! How long has she been out here on this good grass?

He shrugged. "A while, I guess." Then, holding out his arm with the halter, he said, "Here, catch her before she kicks the tar out of this mare."

I walked slowly up to Red and
slipped the halter rope around her neck.
Red turned to sniff me and I gave her a
big hug around her neck. "Hey girl, I'm
back. Did you miss me?" I put the halter
on her head and stepped back to take a
look. I had never seen Red this big.
Something wasn't right. Her body was all
in proportion except her tummy.
Suddenly it hit me. "Russell, is she
pregnant?" The look on his face told me
she was.
"Yep"
"But why?" I whined. "I didn't want
her bred. You know I wanted to train her
this winter for the shows next spring.
That's part of the reason why I went to
England – so I could learn how to train
hunter-jumpers. Now I've got all this
knowledge, and no horse to ride. It really
makes me mad!"
I hauled Red to a nearby tree and
tied her up. Then I went and sat on the
big rock and buried my face in my hands.
I was too angry to cry. Russell was still
sitting on Sunny, holding Figgy by the
bridle reins. He got off and using his
lariat, tied both horses to the same tree.
Then he came over and sat down beside
me.
"Lindz" he said softly. Boy, I hadn't
heard that for a while. It was so much
softer than 'Canada'. "Before you go

getting all upset at me, I want you to know I didn't do it. It was your mom."

"Mom?" I asked. "She never mentioned it in all her letters."

"I know. She wanted it to be a surprise. She figured your mare might as well have a foal. She knows you want to raise horses, and she just thought she would get a jump-start on your breeding program for you." Suddenly, I felt like a fool.

"I'm sorry," I stammered.

"It's okay. I knew you'd be upset at first, but I think you'll be excited to know who the sire is."

"Who? " I was curious now.

"Your mom had Pam make all the arrangements. I had nothing to do with it." Russell pulled a paper out of his jacket pocket and handed it to me. "Here, read this."

It was a photocopy of a pedigree from the Jockey Club of Canada registering the stallion Almighty Dollar, son of Silver Dollar by Pass the Cash by Northern Dancer. "Wow," I said. "This is some impressive pedigree! Silver Dollar won the San Juan Capistrano stakes twice. I didn't know one of his sons was here in Canada."

"Me neither," Russell said. "As I said, I had nothing to do with it." He got up and untied the horses. "Come on, I have to get back. Dad wants me to change the oil in his truck, and I have to do the milking this afternoon. I mounted Figgy. Russell said, "I'll lead Red because she knows Sunny. Those two girls will probably fight. By the way, what do you think of Figgy? Do you like her?"

I leaned over and stroked the mare's mahogany- colored neck. "Yes, I like her fine," I said. She's a lovely horse."

"Well, that's good" Russell grinned, "Because she's yours."

"What? You mean...*I'm* the girl you're keeping her for?"

"Yep. She's a coming home present. I knew you'd need a horse to ride with Red being in foal, and I thought you might want to breed her sometime too. She's got good conformation. She should have nice foals."
Russell's upturned face looked into my own, which was full of surprise. I leaned over to hug him, and he pulled me from the saddle into a tight embrace. "Oh God, Russell, this is just too fantastic to take in!" I said, looking into his eyes. Thank-you so much! I hugged him and kissed him at least a dozen times. "How old is Figgy?" I asked.

"She's nine, and she's had two foals, so breeding her shouldn't be a problem. The kid that owned her belonged to Langley Riders. She rode Figgy in everything; she got ribbons in gymkhana, English and western classes and hunter hack. She showed me all the stuff she won."

I was embarrassed about making a fuss in front of Russell about Redwing being bred. I had just received two wonderful gifts. I contemplated my luck and the future as we rode back down the trail together.

Russell and I had several more rides up to the mountain before the rainy winter season set in. I still rode Redwing around home to keep her relatively fit, but when we went up the mountain I rode Figgy. I grew to love this mare as much as Red. She was so pretty with her Arab looking head. Her dished face, small pointy ears, and her white star and snip set off by large kind eyes made an appealing picture.

In October, I started work as a riding instructor and trainer at the Eagle Ridge Equestrian Center. I didn't have to muck out any stalls, or do any of the heavy lifting or feeding. In the mornings, I worked with young jumping prospects. I used the same techniques that Mark had drilled into us with our young-horse projects. Time and time again, I could 'hear' his voice telling me, "Come on Canada, this is the way we do it over here." I took a break after lunch and usually came home since I was so close.

Later on I went back to give lessons after school and some evenings. My days off were Sunday and Monday. Russell was still working at Buckerfields. He worked Saturdays too, so we usually spent our Sundays together, riding.

On one of our last rides up the mountain, the sky was cerulean blue with big puffy clouds moving lazily across the sky. The maples had donned their glorious autumn colors and the sun-dappled foliage smelled like sweet wine as we passed. When we got to the meadow, we hobbled the horses and let them graze. Russell lay on his back on the faded grass, just looking at the clouds. I joined him, lying so my head was close to his, but our bodies were pointing in different directions.

"What do you see in the clouds...in the future...? I asked. Russell pointed upwards.

"There's a dragon, see? And a waterspout. And over there...look...it's a swan." I had to look hard to see his imaginary figures. "I think I see rings... double rings." He was quiet for a minute. Then as if out of the blue he was so intently looking at, he asked me, "Are you still a virgin?"

The question caught me off guard. I was going to tell him about Mark sometime, but I hadn't planned on it today.

"Nope." I tore off a blade of grass and examined it attentively.

"Neither am I," he said quietly. This news surprised me. *Who? I wondered.*

"Do you want to tell me about it?" he asked.

"Do you really want to know? Are you going to tell *me*?"

"Yeah...I don't think we should have any secrets between us."

"Okay, as long as you don't get all mad and upset."

"I won't. I'll just listen. Go ahead." So I told him about Mark, and how it started when I was a guest at his home for Christmas. I told Russell about what happened that night that he wouldn't speak to me, and of our meetings at Thornhylde.

"That's it?" Russell asked.

"Yes. We really didn't see much of each other privately. We were too busy and our schedules never worked out so that we had time off together."

Russell said, " Did you fall in love with him? "It was a question that I did not know the answer to.

"I might have...or it might have just been infatuation. I liked being with him, and he was very good to me, very generous. He gave me a pearl necklace."

"A *real* one?"

"Yes, a real one."

"Wow, that must have cost a lot."

"Yep. Mark is very wealthy. I'm not sure why he wanted me; he could have any girl he wants."

"That's not hard to figure out."

"Thank-you."

"So, is it over? Are you writing to each other?"

"No, we're not. We'll keep in touch, but as friends. I could have stayed there to work, but I made my choice. I came home... to you."

There was one of those silences that I had forgotten about Russell. It meant he was thinking. I waited. Then I asked him, "What about you?"

He sighed deeply. "That was all a big mistake. Right after you left, I was feeling miserable and hating myself. I went to the bar at the Sportsman's Hotel. It's kind of a dive. I was sitting alone in there, minding my own business when this chick comes up and asks me to dance with her. Well, I didn't want to, but she dragged me up to the dance floor, and I guess I danced a couple with her. We drank some more beer and then she got pretty touchy/feelie with me. I didn't care about anything at that point; not even my own integrity, so I went with her to her place."

That's it?" I asked. "Just the once?"

"Well no, not exactly. I ended up staying with her for three days. I took all my frustrations out on her, and the harder I used her, the more she liked it. Finally I came to my senses and went home. I haven't seen her since."

"Did you even know her name?" I asked.

"Oh yeah, her name was Shelley, or Charlotte, or something like that. It doesn't matter now."

I turned my body around so that I was lying the same way as Russell. I put my arms around him and kissed him. "It doesn't matter about Mark any more either," I told him. "I love you."

He held me tight and said, "I love you too, babe." I would have made love with Russell right then and there, but he showed no indication that he wanted to, so we just stayed where we were holding each other in a loving embrace.

CHAPTER THIRTY-ONE

I guess you could say that Russell and I picked up from where we were in our relationship before I went to England. We did lots of kissing and holding hands, but he never let himself get carried away. We were always in each other's company, yet he conducted himself like a gentleman. He never let his hands go below my waist and he always broke away first if we were getting too passionate with our kisses. It was driving me crazy. I wanted him – all the way, every way, but he had made up his mind and he stuck to it. I had to respect him for that.

In December, not long before Christmas, Russell picked me up from Eagle Ridge. After our kiss of greeting, he said, "I want to show you something, and ask you something. Have you got time to go for a ride into town?"

"Sure," I said, "As long as I don't have to go anywhere fancy in my riding clothes. I smell kind of horsy."

We drove to the mall. It was tough to find a parking place with all the Christmas shoppers. Finally, we drove into a spot that had just been vacated. Russell turned off the ignition and turned to me. He took both of my hands in his, and looked into my eyes. His were so intensely blue...*like that Kingfisher on the water at Thornhylde...Like Mark's... No! I could not think of that now!*

Russell was saying, "And so, will you marry me Linz?"

I gave my head a shake and came back to the present, focusing on those bright blue eyes. Russell's eyes, not Mark's. Mark belonged to another life.

I threw my arms around his neck and squeezed, hard. "Yes!" I said, "Oh yes! When?"

"Oh honey, that's great," he said. "I was thinking of May or June."

"Ooh, that's so far away. I don't think I can wait that long." I said.

"It's only six months. That's not that long to be engaged. He pried me off his chest and neck. "Come on, I want to show you something in the store." I followed him, thinking we were going to pick up something for a celebration meal, but Russell stopped in front of the jewelry store.

"Oh Russell, I can't go in there! I'm such a mess. I've got mud on my boots and I'm covered in horsehair. Let's come back another time, please." I caught at his hand and tried to drag him away.

"Settle down, Lindsey," he said. The ones I like are here in the window. We don't have to go in right now. I just want to show you these."

I relented and let him guide me towards the window where little boxes of matched wedding rings were displayed. "Do you like any of these ones?" he asked. I looked at the rings briefly.

"That one," I said, pointing.

"Good! I've looked at the ones in the store, but these are the ones I liked the best. I was going to surprise you with a ring at Christmas, but then, I thought you'd like to pick your own."

"That so sweet of you," I said as I gave his hand a squeeze. "I like that one because the three diamonds are small and don't stick up. I don't want a ring that will get caught in the horses' manes. And besides, that one has such a distinctive look with those offset ridges. Those are beautiful rings. I'd be proud to wear them."

"Okay, great," he said. "Do you know your ring size?"

"Uh, no, I don't, but here - take this one." He raised his eyebrows at me as I twisted the ring from my finger. "Is it from Mark?"

"No, silly. It's a friendship ring from Joan, one of my room-mates at the school."

"Oh, okay. Sorry for asking." He pocketed the ring.

On Christmas Eve, on my suggestion, Mom had invited The Livingstons over for dessert and coffee. When we had finished, Russell stood up and asked for everyone's attention. He looked at Mom, and his eyes got all misty. "Mrs. Wakefield, he said, "I would like to ask your permission to marry Lindsey. I love her with all my heart. I will take care of her, and be true to her." Mom was only fleetingly surprised and then she smiled happily, went over and hugged Russell, and said, "If Lindsey wants to marry you, then I have no qualms about you two tying the knot. I think we all knew it was just a matter of 'when'."

Russell nodded in agreement and said, "Thank-you." Then he turned to me and kneeled beside the chair where I was sitting. He pulled the ring that we had chosen out of his pocket, and holding it on the flat of his hand, said, "Lindsey, will you take this ring in promise of married life with me?"

I said, "Yes, I'd be honored to wear your ring. I always wanted to marry a cowboy." I blushed as Russell put the diamond ring on my finger and kissed me. Then we were hugging all around the circle. I think all the family was thrilled that we were getting married. Everyone seemed to think that we were made for each other.

The rest of the winter passed in a blur. Russell and I were extremely happy being with each other. We talked a lot about our wedding and set the date for May 30th. I wrote to Mark and told him that I was getting married and invited him to our wedding, as I had promised to do. I never thought for a minute that he would come, but as usual, he surprised me.

I got a phone call from him early one morning, and almost dropped dead when he said he had booked a flight and wanted to attend the wedding! He asked me if I was happy and I said I was. I asked him how his love life was going, and he said, "I'm still looking for the right one. I think I let her slip away." I ignored this comment, and hoped it wouldn't be awkward having him here. Then Mark said, "I'm bringing your wedding present with me. You have to be home when I bring it, because you have to open it right away. It can't wait."

When questioned, he wouldn't give any more clues except that it was big and it was Irish. That definitely got me curious. I said, "Mark, please don't get us something that is terribly extravagant, or costs a fortune. We don't need expensive things, so be reasonable, will you?"

I heard him chuckle as he said, "My fortune is mine to spend as I see fit, so I'm bringing this thing overseas, and I'll no be taking it back!" There was no use arguing with him. I offered to pick him up at the airport but he said, "No, no, don't bother. I want to rent a car so I can travel around and see the countryside. I want to see a rodeo. Are there any on about that time?"

"Yes," I answered, "I think the Cloverdale Rodeo is on then. It's a good one to see. And there are others every weekend throughout the interior of B.C. I'm sure we'll find you a rodeo."

"Okay, then Canada. I can't wait to see you!"

"Me too!" I couldn't tell him that I still longed for his touch and his kisses, even though I was in love with Russell. I said, "Guess what Mark? My dad and his family are coming too. Isn't that great?"

"Hey, that's wonderful news. I'm happy for you Lindsey." We said our goodbyes, and I thought I detected a little twinge of melancholy in his voice. I knew he still missed me too, but there was nothing we could do about it. We had made our choices.

CHAPTER THIRTY-TWO

The invitations were sent out; the church was booked, the food was organized, my dress was ready, and the flowers were all arranged for the wedding.

Mark arrived two days before Russell and I were to be married. He phoned me from the airport, needing directions. I told him how to get to our farm, and then I spent a nervous couple of hours waiting for him. I phoned Russell at work to see if he could get off early and be here when Mark came. Something worried me about being alone with Mark at my house. I didn't want to do anything to jeopardize my marriage now, and I wasn't sure I could resist Mark's Irish charm if he made any advances to me. I felt relieved when Russell said he'd be home in an hour.

Russell and I were out in the garden when a flashy blue sports car turned in at our drive. "That'll be Mark." I said. *God! I was nervous!* Then, behind the car, a truck and horse trailer pulled in. I thought, *what the heck does that guy want – is he lost or something?* I felt annoyed that someone would arrive just as Mark did.

My tall, lanky Irishman got out of the car and came towards me with a jaunty step. He wore jeans, cowboy boots, and a western shirt. He looked so different than how I was used to seeing him, in English jods, high leather boots, and a tweed jacket. He looked just as handsome in western garb as in English though. He enfolded me in a big warm hug, and said, "Ah...Canada...it's good to see you. You're looking bonnie!" He kissed me on the cheek.

I pulled away from his embrace, saying, "I can't believe you came all this way. It's great to see you too!" Then looking at Russell standing there in his work clothes, I said, "Mark, I'd like you to meet Russell." Then to explain his rather messy appearance, I said, "He just got home from work."

"So, you're the Canadian cowboy I've heard so much about. This girl nearly talked my ears off about you, she did." Mark offered his hand and Russell politely shook it. "Nice you could come," he mumbled. I gave him a sharp look. I hoped Russell wasn't going to be rude to Mark after him coming halfway around the world to be at our wedding.

The man in the truck had not gotten out. I said, "Excuse me Mark, but I need to go and see what that man with the horse trailer wants. He's probably looking for the equestrian center. It's just down the road." The three of us walked back to the truck in the driveway. I noticed that both the truck and trailer

had a logo on it saying Lorimer Rentals. I
didn't recognize the young man until he
stepped out of the truck. With a huge grin
he said to me in pure Irish, "Hello
Lindsey, how the devil are ya?"

"Sean!" I yelled, as I threw my arms
around him. "What are you boys up to
now? Mark didn't say you were coming
too! And what are you doing driving
around the country with a horse trailer?"

"Och, you know Mark", he said.
"He'll not tell you the half of it, if he does
na want to. He likes surprises."

"Oh yes, I know that." I said. I took
Sean by the hand and introduced him to
Russell. Just then, the trailer rocked, and I
could hear a horse stamping with
impatience inside.

"Come on then, little brother," Mark
said with an impish grin. "Let's get her
out." Russell and I watched with growing
curiosity as Mark and Sean went to the
back of the trailer and opened the doors.
Mark went in and I heard him talking
soothingly to a nervous horse. It still
hadn't clicked what they were doing.
Then he came down the ramp with a
beautiful dark, iron gray Thoroughbred
filly on the lead line. Still grinning, he
handed me the lead rope as I stared at
the filly. She was a smaller, darker replica
of Desert Wind. She was wide eyed
herself; head up, looking for something
familiar. She spied Redwing and Figgy in

the pasture, and let out a loud bellow of greeting. My two mares responded by galloping over to the fence to see who this new arrival was. I was just starting to figure it out myself.

"Oh my God, Mark!" I said, dumfounded. "This can't be Desert Rose, can it?"

"The very one! You do catch on quick! I would have given you Desert Fire, but a gelding is no good to you if you want to raise horses. I thought this one would be perfect for you, and besides, you named her – she's yours."

You could have knocked me over with a feather as the realization sunk in of the magnitude of Mark's gift. "Oh my God, Mark! What a wonderful gift! This is incredible!" I hugged Mark and Sean all over again, and then I hugged the filly around her neck.

"Oh, Russell! This is so wonderful!" I explained. I rode this filly's dam at Mark's place in Ireland, and I trained her brother Desert Fire at Fulmer. Having her is such a wonderful connection to those great horses."

Russell said, "She sure is a little beauty." We put the filly in the riding ring, where she could touch noses with the mares, but could not be hurt if they decided to bully the younger newcomer. She immediately took off running and bucking, trying to shake off the effects of being confined so long in a small space. Russell went down to the barn to get some hay and water for her. He hadn't said anything in the way of thanks to the brothers for the wonderful gift. I felt angry with him for the first time in ages. I knew what was bugging him. Mark had the audacity to give me a horse for a gift, when Russell had given me one also. It was a case of one- up-man-ship. I broke away from Mark for a moment and went to help Russell with the hay.

"Honey," I said quietly. "I know you're ticked about Mark giving me this filly. She *is* really special to me, but the gift is for *us- for our breeding program.* If you don't show some gratitude and some manners about this, I'll be really angry with you. I mean it!"

Russell looked at me in alarm. I don't think he realized that he was being rude. His clenched jaw softened. "I'm sorry, Babe" he said. "It's hard seeing him here with you, knowing that you two were lovers. Put yourself in my shoes, and think how you would feel if that dame I slept with was here kissing and hugging me, and bringing me an expensive gift."

"Okay, I understand." I sighed, putting my hand on his arm. "Let's just get through the next few days, and then he'll be gone. Just remember, I'm marrying *you,* not *him.* In the meantime, we need to be gracious and polite."

"Okay, I'll do my best." He gave me a semblance of a smile. I leaned over and kissed him on the lips as Mark and Sean joined us at the fence to watch the filly run and play. Fortunately the soft footing of the riding ring and the board fences made for a safe place for her to be turned out in.

Russell then made a point of asking Mark about the transportation requirements and how long it took to get everything in order to ship a horse overseas. Soon he and Mark and Sean were deep in discussion about the vet checks, vaccinations, quarantine, etc. and then I heard Russell say, "Well, this is without a doubt the best and most exciting wedding present we could ever expect. Thank you guys, so much for personally delivering her here." There was much hand shaking and shoulder slapping going on. I breathed a sigh of relief. I stood there and watched Desert Rose as she reared and bucked, flung her pretty head, and cantered around her new home. She was truly a beautiful horse. I was amazed at how my little herd had grown from just one mare to three in only a year. In another month when Redwing foaled, there would be four. It seemed I was on my way to being a horse breeder.

Mark and Sean admired Redwing and My Flair Lady who were also putting on a great show of horseplay for the newcomer. Mark agreed that Figgy looked very much like Tinkerbelle, the Anglo-Arab who was in my string at Fulmer.

I invited Mark and Sean to stay for supper, which they gladly accepted. I wanted Russell to stay too, but he had things to do at home, so he kissed me, said polite goodbyes to the boys, and away he went. Soon, Mom came home from work and we all had a great visit, talking about England, Ireland, Portugal, and of course, horses.

When it was getting late, I apologized for not having room to put them up, but Mark assured me it was no problem to get a motel for a couple of nights. As he was leaving, he said, "I know you're very busy right now, but would you have time to take me for a little ride while I'm here?" I quickly calculated the million and one things I needed to get done before the wedding. And right away, I put riding with Mark at the top of the list.

"If you can come back in the morning, I could take you then. Later in the day, my sister and family are arriving from the states, and dad will be coming tomorrow night. We have a rehearsal tomorrow too."

"Tomorrow morning would be perfect," he said. Sean is going to take the truck and trailer back to Vancouver, and I need to pick him up about noon."

"Okay, see you about nine o'clock,"
I said. I was glad Mom had gone to bed.
She would have skinned me alive if she
knew I was going riding in the morning,
with so much to do. "Goodnight Sean.
Goodnight Mark. Thanks again for such a
wonderful surprise."

"Goodnight Lindsey, they both said,
as they kissed and hugged me. Mark held
me in his arms just a little too long. I
broke the embrace, and stepped back.

"See you in the morning," I said.

CHAPTER THIRTY-THREE

I was glad that Mom and Russell were at work. I don't know why I felt so guilty about going riding with Mark the day before my wedding. It seemed perfectly innocent – two old friends doing what they love best – riding horses. We hadn't had a chance to visit alone since he arrived, so I think both of us just wanted the chance to talk. At least, that's what I told myself.

I saddled Figgy for Mark and he adjusted the stirrups to fit his long legs. He gave me a leg up on Red. I was riding her bareback. She was heavy in foal, so I told Mark that we could not go for very long or go fast.

We headed out through the back gate and onto the dyke that wound alongside the Fraser River. Already the sun was hot.

Russell and I were going horse camping up in Manning Park for our honeymoon, so I was telling Mark about our preparations. He was intrigued that we wanted to do something like that. He thought we'd be going to some exotic place like Hawaii. We were riding side by side, with our legs almost touching. Mark asked me, "So how's it really going with your cowboy? Does he make you happy?"

"Of course we're happy," I said. "We're getting married, aren't we?"

"That's not what I mean...how's it going...you know...in the sack?"

I blushed and stammered, "Mark! That's really none of your business!"

He gave that easy laugh of his and reached over and took my free hand. "Just curious, Canada. Don't have a hissy fit." We were silent for a while, and then he said," Would you believe me if I told you that I haven't slept with anyone since you left?"

I was genuinely surprised. I said, "I would find that hard to believe. A man of your talents should have no trouble finding another bed partner."

Mark looked at me seriously. "Oh aye," he said. "They're all around, but I don't want anyone but you. You're all I've been thinking of these past eight months." Then, before I could think of an answer, Mark did something so quick and easy- like I hardly saw him do it. He kicked his feet out of the stirrups, pushed up on the pommel of the saddle with his strong arms, and vaulted onto Redwings back, right behind me. She jumped in surprise as the extra weight landed on her back, but Mark hung on tightly to my waist and she continued to walk sedately on.

"Mark!" What are you doing? Get off!" I tried to pry his hands off and dig him in the ribs with my elbows, but he just laughed at me. He ran his fingers down my thighs, squeezing gently and then his hands were inside my shirt touching my bare skin. He moved my hair aside and kissed me on the neck and ears. I felt like I was a piece of sweet and sticky butterscotch melting in the sunshine. I leaned back into him and the weight that was pushing against me as we kissed. It felt so...good! . Redwing stopped as our combined weight shifted backwards, and we practically fell off the horse in a tangle of arms and legs. Figgy had already stopped and was grazing the lush grass in the ditch, her bridle reins dragging. "Mark..." I protested weakly as he pulled me by the hand down the bank to the shade of some trees. "I can't do this! I'm getting married tomorrow! Stop it!"

He laid me down and pulled me against him. "Are you on the pill?" he asked me.

"Yes, I am...but"...my words trailed off as he covered me with kisses. I could resist no longer. We laid there in the shade making love, and I totally forgot that I would be another man's bride tomorrow night. Mark had that kind of effect on me. When I was with him, I was crazy about him. When I was away from him, I wanted Russell.

It was cool in the shade. Mark and I sat up and put our clothes back on. As Mark ran his fingers through my hair, I told him, " Russell and I...we haven't made love yet. We're waiting till we're married."

Mark gave me an incredulous look. "Why not?" he said. "Now, I find *that* hard to believe. What's the matter with him?"

"It's true. Russell said in his letter that he'd be here for me as a friend or *more*, if I want. Well, I think we proved the friendship thing, and I've wanted the *more* for a long time, but he keeps putting me off. He's the one that wanted to wait, so I went along with it. I know it all goes back to our near breakup last summer and he's just trying to prove that he's grown up now and is in control of his emotions. I think it's very noble of him."

"Well, I think he's daft! I don't see how he could resist you...you are so beautiful, and sexy. I love you." He bent his head for another long kiss.

I groaned and tried to push him away half-heartedly. "Mark, why didn't you tell me before this? It could have changed everything. I told you I loved you a long time ago, but you didn't say you loved me back. It's too late now."

Mark said softly, "I know it's too late, and I'm sorry for that. I didn't know myself when you left if I loved you or not, but I went back to Thornhylde and spent some time there by myself. I missed you so much, and it became clear to me that I wanted you there with me. I was just kicking myself for letting you go. I wish I had asked you to stay and share my life with me then."

"I wish you had too," I said. "I can't change things now, or at least I won't. I wouldn't do that to Russell. I love him too."

We caught up the horses and headed back. We turned the mares out in the pasture, and then it was time for Mark to go. We held each other for several minutes. He was close to tears when he said, "I wish you every happiness, my darling. If you ever need me, or if I can help you in any way, please, just ask." He kissed me lightly. "I won't do anything to get in your way tomorrow," he said. "I just want you to be happy."

I just nodded, and waved goodbye. I was too overwhelmed with emotion to say anything.

It's a good thing I was so busy for the rest of the time right up to the wedding. I didn't have a spare minute to dwell upon Mark or what we had done. The church was full. When the Wedding March started, I kept my eyes and thoughts on Russell waiting for me as I walked slowly down the aisle on my dad's arm. Dad, Jenny and Percy had arrived from England the night before. My sister Sarah and husband Steven had come from the U.S. I hadn't seen them in four years so we had a lot of catching up to do. Russell's brother Danny was standing up with Russell as best man. His wife Pat was sitting with Mom and Victoria Donnelley. My sister Maryanne was my Maid of Honor. All my family was sitting teary eyed in the front row. A handful of Abbey High kids, Russell's rodeo friends, and our bus driver, Mrs. Klein, had come. Mom was pleasant to my dad, but I'm sure it was hard for her. She surprised me by inviting Paul Hanson, her friend that she had met on the ship. He was from Seattle, Washington. Paul was a widower, about ten years older than Mom, with white hair and moustache, and soft, brown eyes. His wife had died of cancer a couple of years ago. Since Mom was a nurse, Paul had felt comfortable talking to her about his wife's illness. She understood all that hospital lingo. I was happy to see she had a man-friend at long last. They had been writing to each other since Mom had arrived home, but this was the first time they had got together. They seemed to be getting along very well.

I felt like one special gal having all these people come to see me marry my high school sweetheart. But, as I exchanged my vows with Russell, a microscopic part of Mark was working its magic way down deep inside me. He had planted a seed that would change the course of my life. I was pregnant.

CHAPTER THIRTY-FOUR

Our wedding was beautiful, and everything went smoothly. I was so relieved when the ceremony was finally over. Even though he had promised, I was terrified that Mark would stand up and say something when it came to that time when the minister asked; "Can anyone show just cause why these two should not be joined in marriage?" It was good that I had my back to the congregation. I could not have faced Mark, or my family after what I had done yesterday.

We had a catered roast beef dinner at the church hall, all the usual speeches, receiving line, the cutting and delivering of the pieces of cake, and then I threw my bouquet over my shoulder. I know I was blushing when Mark kissed me and wished me good luck in the receiving line, but then, brides are supposed to blush, so I got away with that one.

Instead of a dance, we had an open house at the Livingston farm, so that people from out of town, and in particular our Irish and English guests could visit and get to know each other. Dad spent some serious time getting re-acquainted with his two daughters. I was happy to see that was going well. Percy was having fun with his cousins, Jesse and Luke. Dad also enjoyed meeting and talking with the

McTaggart brothers. Russell was quiet and it took a while to get to know him, but Mark and his brother Sean were outgoing and gregarious; interested in everybody and everything. They were excited about going to see their first rodeo the next day. When they left, just before midnight, Russell and I stood side by side and thanked them profusely for coming, and once again for bringing Desert Rose. There were hugs and hand shakes and wishes of good luck for a happy life together, and then Mark was gone out of my life again. I steeled myself against the pain I felt, watching him stride away with a cheerfulness I know he didn't feel. I found out several years later that he had got good and drunk that night so he could blot out the vision of Russell and I sleeping together.

Russell had set our tent up in the back yard, and had made our marriage bed cozy with double foamies and warm sleeping bags. When he came to me, I held him tight and loved him well. Afterwards, I wept a little, and told him they were tears of joy. In part, that was true, but they were also shed for the one I loved and could not have.

When we came into the farmhouse the next morning for a breakfast of pancakes, eggs, and bacon, Ben gave us a wink and asked if we had slept well.

"Hell no, dad," Russell grinned. "Who sleeps on their wedding night?" I stared into my coffee cup, with a dreamy smile on my face, not saying a word. I didn't want to get into this conversation.

We left that morning, and set up our camp in a wilderness area of Manning Provincial Park. Our days were spent on long, scenic trail rides on Sunny and Figgy. It was so easy being with Russell; we didn't have to talk much. At night, we cooked delicious meals over an open fire. We'd sit close, watching the meteorites blazing through the starry heavens, and when we started to get cold and tired, we'd go cuddle up in the tent and warm each other up.

On the last day, when we were breaking camp, Russell was rolling up the sleeping bags, and I was packing my clothes into my backpack, when I happened to discover an object in the bottom of my bag. I said to Russell, "Hey, did you buy me this? I haven't seen it before."

"What is it? he asked. I held up the little statue. I was surprised to see it was a miniature ceramic leprechaun. The little figure was clad in green overalls, beige shirt with green shamrock buttons, and a green Tamo-shanter on his shaggy, pointy-eared head. Across the bottom, in small letters, it read: 'Anything can happen.' We both stared at the thing in amazement. "Where did that come from?" Russell asked me.

"I don't have any idea how it got in my bag, but it had to have been Mark that did it," I said. He must have slipped out to the tent when no one was looking. My bag was out there. That Irish devil!" I laughed. "He sure enjoys a joke. He loves to tease." I could see that Russell was not impressed with Mark and his jokes, so I tucked the little fellow back into my bag. Much later, long after I had given birth to Kaitlyn, I pondered about that little mischief-maker being with us on our honeymoon, without our knowledge.

Russell and I settled easily and happily into married life. It really wasn't much different than before, except that we now had a love life, and it was good. He worked full time at Buckerfields Livestock and Feed Company, and I kept on with my teaching and training at Eagle Ridge Equestrian Center. My mom moved back into the apartment she had when she returned from her trip, so that Russell could move in with me. We were buying the property from her. Russell was going to take over his father's land and dairy business when Ben retired in a few years. We had plans to move a new modular home onto our five acres, and then sell the little place when we made the move to the Livingston farm. Russell felt that the old house wasn't worth fixing up any more, and he had concerns about the wiring and cracks in the basement wall.

Three weeks after our wedding, Redwing gave birth to a healthy chestnut colt. I was with her for the entire process, but she didn't need any help. I got my hands on the colt before he even got up, touching him all over his body, so he would accept humans. He had a large star, strip and snip of white on his cute face, and two white hind socks. He was going to be a flashy looking gelding some day. When Russell got home from work I took him down to the barn to see the new baby. He asked me, " That's a nice colt. What are you going to call him?"

I said, " Since his dam is 'Doc's Dancing Doll' and his sire 'Almighty Dollar', I was thinking of 'Dollar Bill.'"

Russell grinned and said, "Sure! " So the name stuck, and we called him 'Willy' for short.

Everything was going great until I started to feel sick every morning. Pregnancy never crossed my mind. I was on the pill and I was too busy to think about having a baby yet. Whatever mysterious malady I had seemed to bother me the most when I first got up. After I had eaten something, I felt better, so I just ignored it and carried on with my work. Russell heard me throwing up a few times, and urged me to see a doctor.

When I missed my period, I began to think something was wrong, but I still didn't think I was pregnant. The bouts of sickness got worse and came throughout the day as well as in the morning. I couldn't get through teaching a lesson without running out to throw up, and my energy and tolerance level diminished rapidly when I was training young horses. The motion of riding made me sick, and I seemed to have no strength. In desperation I went to my doctor. She gave me news I did not want to hear.

"Congratulations, Lindsey," she said cheerfully. "You are in the family way. Your baby will be born in February or early March."

"But I *can't* be!" I said. "I've been taking my pills regularly! I've only been married for two months. I *don't want* to be pregnant!" I started to cry. The doctor was sympathetic and changed her tone from being jolly to concerned. She put her arm around me in a friendly fashion. "I'm sorry, you're upset, Lindsey. We started you on a very low dose. It's usually enough to protect against pregnancy. However, they are not one hundred percent foolproof. Sometimes there is a breakthrough, and it does say on the package to use a backup form of

contraceptive during the first week. Did
you?"

"No." I sniffed.

" I'm afraid that your healthy body
just decided it wasn't going to let any old
drug get in the way of Mother Nature."
The doctor paused. "Do you have a faith,
Lindsey?"

I looked up at her in surprise. I
nodded. "I went to Sunday School. I
believe in God."

"Well, that's good," said the Doctor.
Sometimes these things happen for a
purpose, despite all the odds. Sometimes
that purpose is kept hidden from us for a
while. I think that when you adjust to
having this baby, you will find peace and
happiness." She gave me a big smile of
encouragement.

"I hope you're right," I said as I rose
to leave her office. I went out to the
parking lot and got into Pam's truck that I
had borrowed for my appointment. I put
my head down on my crossed arms over
the steering wheel and wept bitter tears.
"I don't want a baby." I wailed. I wanted to
ride and train and show the horses I was
working with. I wanted a chance to apply
the lessons I learned at Fulmer. "Damn
stupid useless pills!" I shouted. I worked
myself into such a tizzy that I felt I had to
throw up. I went around to the back of
the truck and heaved my meager lunch,

cursing this 'thing' that was making me
sick. Then the thought hit me!
*Could this be Mark's child? Oh
God, yes! It could be! What if it had
flaming red hair and looked exactly like
Mark? It would break Russell's heart if he
knew that I had been with Mark the day
before our wedding.*

I thought about getting rid of it;
talking to the doctor and begging her to
let me have an abortion. I knew there had
to be grounds for qualifying for abortion.
You had to be mentally insane, or the
victim of rape, or some such thing. I knew
I couldn't hide it from Russell any longer,
and I also knew that he would have an
absolute fit if I wanted an abortion. I felt
trapped and miserable.

I drove slowly back to the arena
where Pam was teaching my lesson for
me in my absence. She spotted me
standing by the rail, and came over. "Hey,
Lindsey! Everything all right? Oh, God,
you look awful! What's wrong?"

I heaved a great sigh. "I'm
pregnant, Pam. And I don't want to be.
What can I do?" I looked at her
desperately. Pam gave me a weird look.

"Oh no, I can't do anything to help
you," she said. "Even if it wasn't planned,
it was meant to be Lindsey. You have to
accept it." She gave me an encouraging
grin. "The first three months are the

worst for being sick; after that it's not so
bad."

"Yeah, and after that you get fat
and awkward, and have heartburn and
piles. I know...my sister has kids." I was
feeling sorry for myself.

Pam looked over at the students in
the arena. "I've got to finish this lesson.
Go on into my office and we'll talk there.
See you in a bit."

"Okay, thanks Pam". I turned to go,
and there was Russell coming towards
me.

"Hi sweetie," he said. I finished up
early today, so I came to pick you up.
How's everything?" Then he caught a look
at my tear-stained face and concern lined
his own. "What's going on?" he said. "Are
you hurt? Why is Pam teaching your
lesson?" He put his arms around me and
pulled me against his chest. I started to
cry again. He called out to Pam; "I'm
taking Lindsey home." Pam gave him the
thumbs up sign as we headed out to the
truck.

"For God's sake, Lindsey, tell me
what's the matter," Russell said as he
held the truck door open for me. I
climbed in and waited until he came
around and got in on his side. "Talk to
me, Lindsey," he said.

"I'm bloody pregnant!" I shouted
through my tears. I felt immediately sorry
for yelling when I looked at Russell's hurt

and shocked expression. I tried to explain. "The pills...it was during the first week. We were supposed to use backup contraception during the first week...I didn't read all of the information...apparently they're not 100% reliable...so I got caught." I sobbed out the story.

Russell put his arms around me. I let myself be held and comforted. "Sh...it's gonna be okay, honey. We'll manage. You don't have to work if it's too hard. Take a year off. It doesn't matter."

It *does* matter! I spent a year overseas working my butt off to learn how to teach riding and train horses, and now I'm being forced out of my job because of this...this...*thing* that's growing in me!"

"Hey, Lindsey...calm down," Russell said. He held me close, kissing me on my wet cheek. "I know we didn't want kids for a few years, but we can handle this. I'll help you as much as I can, okay?" And our moms are here to help out too. It won't be so bad, you'll see." I was not convinced.

CHAPTER THIRTY-FIVE

The summer seemed to drag by. I was hot and uncomfortable most of the time. If I stood too long, my back ached; if I sat too long, I had to go to the bathroom, if I lay down for a rest, I'd get cramps in my feet or legs. I just plain hated being pregnant. I resented the baby for taking away my freedom, and I was constantly worried that it would look enough like Mark to arouse suspicion.

Russell was wonderfully supportive, and I really tried hard not to complain and be crabby when he was home. As I increased in size, he got more and more excited about the baby. He completely re-did my mom's old room with new paint and cute wallpaper and a new rug on the floor. We bought a crib and change table and a few blankets and outfits. My sister had lots of baby clothes stored away; so she told me not to get carried away with buying a lot of stuff.

Reluctantly, I quit working at the stable. I found that just taking care of my own small herd, looking after the garden and preparing Russell's meals was enough to drain my energy for the day. I still rode occasionally, but didn't gallop or jump. I'd saddle Sunny or Figgy and just ride quietly down the dykes for an hour or two.

266

I halter broke Willy and sometimes ponied him from Redwing. He was the typical stud colt – full of mischief and testosterone. He liked to rear and strike and bite, and I had to handle him carefully, lest he knock me over with his exuberance. I knew I would have to either sell him or geld him before he was a year old. I toyed briefly with the idea of keeping him a stallion, so I could breed him to Desert Rose and Figgy, but we weren't set up to handle a stallion, and besides, he would have to be trained for either a racing or show career before anyone would bring their mares for breeding. With a new baby to look after, I knew I wouldn't have the time to put into his training.

At Christmas, we received a generic letter from Mark wishing us both a happy Christmas. He was living at Thornhylde now. There were two boys and two girls as students this year at Fulmer, and Liz had wanted the cottage for the boys. The girls were in Bredalbane House.
He wrote that he was having a barn built, and putting in a riding ring and paddocks so that he could bring Merlin and Desert Fire there. He told me he had decided to keep the gray gelding, rather than find a buyer for him. I learned later, that he wanted the colt because I had trained him, and it was a way of staying connected to me. There was no mention

of a girlfriend in his letter. I wrote in my Christmas card to him that we were expecting a baby in February or early March. I left it for him to do the math as to when I conceived.

The day I went into labor, March 2nd, was windy and cold. I had felt restless all day. Despite the chill in the air, I saddled Figgy and went for a short ride. My back ached and riding didn't help. Being around the horses always lifted my spirits, so I spent some time brushing the winter hair from their coats, and picking up horse buns with the manure fork. I tried to ignore the crampy feeling I was getting every now and then. When I came in to shower off the horsehair and manure smell, I realized that I was in the early stages of labor. A feeling of tremendous excitement and relief flooded over me. At last I would be free of this burden I was carrying!

When Russell came home from work and I told him I was having contractions, he was so excited he could hardly eat his dinner. He wanted to time the contractions, and asked me over and over if I was ready to go to the hospital. Finally when they were two to three minutes apart, I said,
"Let's go!"

What followed was the most bone-crunching, mind boggling, body-splitting torture I could ever have imagined. *How could there be so many people in the world if giving birth was this horrible?* Russell was by my side helping me through each stage of the birth. My doctor and the nurse kept on saying that this was a normal birth and everything was coming along beautifully. Well, if that was a normal birth, I guess I was thankful that it didn't go on any longer than it did. Finally it was time to give the big 'heave-ho' and push it out. I almost passed out with the effort, but I heard Russell telling me it was a girl. The first thing I asked him was, "What color is her hair?" And then I blacked out.

When I came to a short time later, the nurses had cleaned me up and moved me to a room by myself. I opened my eyes to see Russell by the bed holding the swaddled infant in his arms. He had a goofy look of pride and joy on his face, as if he had given birth to her himself. "Hi honey," he grinned. "Look what we have. A beautiful little girl!" There was no mistaking the delight he felt. I struggled to sit up as he brought the baby to me and tucked her into my arms. I looked down at her little face, all pink and rosy, trying to see whom she resembled. Thank God her hair wasn't red; it was just blonde fuzz. I could live with that. She could be anybody's child, but I hoped to God that Russell was her father. Tears of relief rolled down my cheeks. I didn't feel that surge of a mother's love that was supposed to happen. Oh well, I was tired out now...maybe it would come later.

I wanted to name the baby Lorena, after Mark's sister that I had so much fun with that night at the ceilidh, but I didn't dare tell Russell. He wanted to call her Kaitlyn, so I agreed to that. Things went pretty well in hospital with the nurses there to care for the baby, and I had lots of visitors too. But when I went home, and the baby showers were over, and the excitement died down and I was left alone with her, I felt very lonesome and sad. When people like my family or friends were around, I tried to look happy about the baby. When I was alone with her, I cried a lot. I took good care of her, and wouldn't do anything to harm her, but I just didn't feel that close bond everyone talked about between mother and child. I know now what I was going through was post partum depression, but at the time I wasn't aware that such a condition existed. It's a wonder my mom, being a nurse, didn't pick up on it. I was pretty good at hiding it when anyone was around, except Russell. He got the brunt of it. Sometimes when he'd come home from work after hauling heavy feed bags around all day, I wouldn't even have the breakfast dishes done, and no supper was on the table. Sometimes he'd find me

270

down in the barn, completely unaware of
what time it was. I would have Kaitlyn
with me in her snuggli, but I'd just be
brushing the horses or some useless
thing. There were days when I couldn't be
bothered to have a shower or wash my
greasy hair. I slept when the baby slept,
and could not seem to get enough rest.

Russell took over more and more
care of the baby in the evenings. He was
crazy about her and he loved playing with
her, bathing her, rocking her to sleep,
and tucking her into bed.

When I had healed up and Russell
wanted to resume our love life, I wasn't
very co-operative. I did my duty, but I
wasn't a very fun partner. He was quite
patient with me though all of this, but at
times he got angry at me and yelled at
me to get a hold of myself, get off my
ass, and start behaving like a wife and
mother.

What should have been a blissful first
year of marriage was not very happy, and
I subconsciously blamed Kaitlyn for
wrecking everything. She came between
my relationship with Russell, and my
ability to work with the horses, both at
home and on the job. The other thing
was, that as she outgrew the infant stage
and became a toddler, her hair took on a
beautiful coppery-blond color and I was
almost certain I could see traits of Mark

in her. The way she smiled – that wide, lopsided kind of grin, and something in the shape and color of her eyes constantly reminded me of an Irish imp. I was so afraid that others would see it too. If anyone commented on whom she looked like, I would try to change the subject and say, "Oh she is just herself!"

By the time spring approached and Kaitlyn had her first birthday; I was gradually coming out of my depression. At Katie's party, surrounded by family, I realized that I was very well off. I had a young, handsome husband that loved me, a beautiful, healthy daughter; two doting grandmothers and a grand-dad that were always happy to baby-sit if I wanted to go out for a ride; I had four fine-looking horses; I didn't have to go to work to put food on the table, and I had a nice home. I had so much to be thankful for, and I made a conscious decision to make it up to Russell and Kaitlyn for my lack of attention.

Russell and I celebrated our second anniversary at the end of May. He wined and dined me, while his mom looked after Kaitlyn. That night as I lay in his arms, I talked to him about how hard these past two years had been for us. I told him that I loved him, and I promised that the next year was going to be so much better. I didn't have much of a chance to prove it. Just two weeks later, disaster struck.

CHAPTER THIRTY-SIX

Kaitlyn usually slept for two hours in the afternoon. As the days got longer, and the green grass and plants started to grow, I began going outside to work in the garden or do some training with the horses while she slept. Willy had been gelded, so that he could be turned out in the pasture with the mares.

It was a Saturday, June the 17th. Russell was over at the dairy farm, swathing hay in the field while Ben baled. It was perfect haying weather; not a cloud in the sky and no rain in the forecast. I had made a chicken casserole, which I was going to take over to the farm for supper. The men would be out working in the fields all day and would be hungry and tired when they came in. I put Kaitlyn down for her nap, and then hurried down to the basement and threw a load of wet clothes into the dryer. Then I went out to catch Redwing. I hadn't ridden her in quite a while. I saddled her and brought her up to the riding ring, thinking about getting started on Desert Rose's training soon. She was a three-year-old now and ready for her first lessons under saddle. But today was so beautiful; I just wanted to have a fun ride and not do anything serious. I trotted Redwing around the ring a few times and put her over some small

274

jumps. I didn't feel like training today. I just wanted to go for a pleasure ride. I had always stayed close when Katie was asleep, but I didn't think it would matter if I just rode down the dyke a little ways. I wouldn't be gone long, and she wasn't due to wake up for another hour. Just to make sure, I went into the house and peeped into her room. Yes, she was sleeping soundly. I went back out, mounted Red and headed out the back gate and up the bank to the dyke.

I was mindful of the time as I cantered Redwing along the grassy path. She was happy to get out too; we hadn't been out for a run for a long time. I took her down to the river, let the reins loose and let her drink and crop some of the fresh sweet grass along the riverbank. In half an hour, I reluctantly turned her head for home.

As soon as we came up from the river onto the dyke I could smell smoke. I wasn't too alarmed; there were lots of people burning old grass and rubbish at this time of year. But when I rounded the bend my heart felt like it had stopped in my chest! An agonized cry escaped from my throat as I screamed to Red, "Our house is on fire! Run Red!" I slammed my heels into her sides and leaned over her neck as she jumped into a gallop. Red seemed to feel the urgency in my body and my voice as I pleaded with her to run her best race ever. She flattened out and galloped at top speed. I cried, "Oh God, Oh God, Oh God, spare my Kaitlyn, spare my baby!"

Red slowed for the sharp turn down the bank. We usually stopped to open the gate, but I hammered her with my heels and yelled at her, "Jump Red! We haven't got time for the gate!" Redwing bounced down the bank in two strides, gathered herself and leaped over the four-foot gate with room to spare. She landed galloping hard and headed straight for the barn. Frantically, I pulled the right rein, heading her up the pasture for the house. I could now see the smoke billowing out of the windows, and flames licking the walls. At the same time I saw Russell's truck in a cloud of dust, heading up the driveway at breakneck speed. I sawed Redwing to a halt and jumped off her right side. She veered away and ran back to the barn. I plunged into the horse's watering trough, soaking myself and then vaulted the gate that led to the yard. I entered the house running.

Russell was already there ahead of me. As I entered the living room I was met with thick, black choking smoke. I dropped to my knees and crawled in the direction of the back bedroom, calling "Russell – get Katie!" I couldn't see anything. Then I found myself at the bedroom door. It was ablaze, and just

inside I could see the shadow of Russell
with the baby in his arms. I stood up.
"Russell!" I screamed.
"Lindsey!" he shouted. "I'm going to
throw her to you!" He had wrapped her in
a blanket to protect her from the fire and
smoke. There was a wall of fire between
us, but I yelled back, "Throw her! I'll catch
her!"
The bundle came hurtling through
the smoke and ash. I caught her, and
turned to run, thinking Russell was
coming right behind me. When I
staggered out into the fresh air,
coughing, the yard was filling with
people. The neighbors had come as well
as two fire trucks and an ambulance. Two
ladies ran up and grabbed me and took
Kaitlyn from my arms. She was wiggling,
so I knew she was alive. "Russell's in
there"...I managed to cough out." I
wrenched myself away from the well-
meaning arms and ran back in, calling for
Russell. Two firemen, trying to hook up
their hoses, called out for me to stop, but
I ignored them. I had to see where Russell
was! I crawled in again, under the thick
black smoke and made my way to the
bedroom.
I found Russell, just outside the
bedroom in the hallway. He was slumped
on the floor with the burning doorjamb
over his back. I screamed and pulled the
burning timber off him; never even

feeling my hands touch the fire. I grabbed him by the shirt and tried to drag him out. He was so heavy! Almost immediately, the two firemen were at my side; one pulling me towards fresh air, and the other dragging Russell's inert body out. The man dropped me on the grass where I lay choking and coughing. He ran to assist the other fireman. I saw them roll Russell over and over to squelch his burning clothes, and I heard them calling for oxygen and a stretcher. After that, everything was a blur. Marcie and Ben found me and I gasped out that I was okay, that Katie was out, but that Russell was hurt. They hurried away to find him. I heard the ambulance screaming away, and then two paramedics picked me up and helped me to the back of a van. One of them said, "We've got to get those hands tended to." I still didn't realize that my hands had been burned trying to rescue Russell. I could hardly speak because of the smoke I had inhaled. My voice came out in a squeak as I asked, over and over again where Russell was, and if he was all right. And where was Kaitlyn? I didn't know if she was hurt. If she wasn't burned or damaged by smoke inhalation, I knew she would at least be terrified. I started to get hysterical when these people wouldn't give me any answers. "I want my baby! I want my husband!" I screamed.

"Look, lady, they've been taken care of," the young fellow said. "I'll get on the radio and find out where they are and what their condition is, okay? Just give us a minute to get your hands bandaged. They're badly burned."

"Are they?" I looked at my hands in amazement as the paramedic spread some kind of thick cream on them and proceeded to wrap them with gauze. I tried to co-operate as he worked on my blistered hands, but I was in shock and couldn't stop sobbing and asking for Russell repeatedly. The younger of the two went to the front of the van and radioed the ambulance. He spoke into the black receiver, "027, Ron here...what's the condition of the patient?" There was a pause. "We've got his wife here...serious burns and smoke inhalation." Then, "Okay, where's the baby?...Yep. Got it. Thanks 027 out."

He came back and said to me, "Your husband has some severe burns. He's in the ambulance on his way to emergency. They're giving him oxygen and trying to stabilize him." I jumped up. "I need to be with him!"

Ron said, "We'll take you there right away. Your daughter has also been taken to emergency by the grandparents. She is traumatized and suffered some smoke inhalation, but she'll be okay." I managed to mumble a hoarse 'thank-you'. They were doing their best to get everyone looked after. As we swept out of the driveway past the crowd that had gathered, I took one last look at the little house that was now completely engulfed in flames. There would be nothing salvaged. I knew that Buck was safe because he had been with me on the ride. I couldn't remember if Ying Yang was in the house or not. I prayed she was out. I knew the neighbors would watch out for them, and I hoped that someone would look after Redwing, who still had her saddle and bridle on.

When we got to the hospital, we were told that Russell had been rushed to O.R. The doctor on call took one look at me and ordered me admitted as well. My eyebrows were gone, my face was blistered, and my body was beginning to register the pain that the burns had caused. Marcie and Ben were in emergency with Katie, and she was howling. They were frantic about Russell. Kaitlyn was wild eyed, and crying, but she was safe. Her daddy had rescued her just in time. She clung to me and I held her as tightly as I could with my bandaged hands. Marcie told me she had phoned my mom, and that she was on her way. There was nothing we could do but wait for news of Russell's condition.

Mrs. Williams, my neighbor that had taken Kaitlyn from my arms when I stumbled out of the burning house, arrived at the hospital to see what she could do to help. The doctor said that Kaitlyn was going to be fine, so Mrs. Williams took her home.

A nurse helped me out of my wet and singed clothing, and took me by wheelchair to a bed in the burn unit. When the pain from the burns on my face and hands increased, a nurse came and gave me a shot that deadened the emotional and physical agony somewhat. I floated in and out of consciousness, crying for Russell every time I came to. Finally, I slept.

A while later, I woke up with a start to see Mom beside my bed. She looked terrible; haunted and sad. I must have looked terrible too. My face had swollen and blistered; my eyes were almost sealed shut, my lips were raw, and my hands ached. "Mom", I squeaked out... "Russell?"

Mom's eyes filled with tears as she rose and put her arms around me. "Russell didn't make it honey...I'm so sorry. They tried so hard to save him."

"Oh no!" I cried. "No!" I pushed Mom away and crumpled down into my bed, turning on my side to hide my face. My body shook with sobs. My blistered and burned face stung with the tears that flowed out of my swollen eyes. I wailed as loud as my hoarse voice would allow, "Why didn't they let me go with him? Oh...why wasn't I with him? Oh Russell! My beloved! You can't be gone! No!"

Mom just let me rant and rave and cry until I got over the worst of it. Then she tried to explain. "Lindsey, there was so much confusion at the fire, the ambulance attendants didn't know you were his wife. They knew the paramedics were giving you first aid, and they did what they thought best, and that was to get Russell to emergency as soon as possible."

"I want to see him," I said through my tears. "I need to talk to him; there's so much I have to tell him."

"We'll have to ask the doctor if you can. "I'm sure she can arrange it". Mom wiped my face gently with a cool cloth. It felt good. I turned so she could do the other side." Where are Marcie and Ben?" I asked. My head felt like it was spitting open.

"They're down in one of the parents' rooms. They're taking it pretty hard".

"How long ago did he die?" My voice came out in a whisper.

"About an hour ago," Mom said. "They did everything they possibly could to keep him alive."

"Why was I allowed to go to sleep?" I wailed again. "I should have been with him! I was sleeping, while he was dying! That's just unfair!" I covered my face with my bandaged hands and had another crying jag.

There was a knock on the door, and Russell's parents came into the room. I sat up on the edge of my bed and held them both in my embrace. All four of us were crying. They were shocked at my appearance, but they were more devastated by the tragic loss of their son. We were all in a state of shock and sorrow.

Mom went out to the nursing station and asked if we could see the doctor. In a little while she came in, saying how sorry she was for our loss. She checked my face and hands. I asked her if we could see Russell, and she replied, "He was very badly burned. You might not want to see him. It might be too upsetting for you."

"I want to see him," I said stubbornly. " I didn't get a chance to say goodbye."

Ben said that they wanted to see their son too, and so it was arranged. I was so shaky and couldn't see well, so Mom pushed me in a wheelchair. A nurse and an orderly came with us down to the basement. They asked us to wait in a small room, and then the orderly went to get the body. He wheeled Russell out into the hallway on a gurney, and pulled the sheet that was covering him off. Then he opened the door to the room, and nodded at us, moving away discreetly. Ben and Marcie went first. They came back, crying, in about ten minutes. Then it was my turn. Mom wheeled me out into the dimly lit hallway and parked me beside Russell's body. He was lying on his left side. Mom put her hand on his head as if in blessing, and said, "Go with God...know that we all love you." Then she left me alone. I was shaking so hard I could hardly stand up. The O.R. staff had removed Russell's shirt. His back and shoulders were criss-crossed with angry red welts from where the burning beams had fallen across him. The left side of his face was untouched where it must have been lying across his arm, but the right side was charred and shriveled like shoe leather. The eye was sunken. His thick, brown curls were all but gone; burned to a crisp. His mouth was twisted in a grimace of pain. I realized that had he lived, his recovery would have been slow and excruciating. He would have been blind in one eye, and scarred. In dying he had been spared many months of painful rehabilitation. Even though I was shocked and devastated by his death, I felt relieved that he would not have to suffer any more.

I reached out with a bandaged
finger and touched those lips that I had
kissed so many times. I held his hands in
my painful ones, thinking of how those
dear hands had caressed me in love; how
they had soothed and comforted Kaitlyn;
how fine and light they were on the reins
of his beloved Sundance; how capable
those hands were milking a cow or fixing
an engine that wouldn't run. With tears
spilling down my red face, I said to him,
"Russell... I love you so much. It's my
fault you died. It should have been me
that died in the fire. I left Kaitlyn alone.
She's not even your daughter. She's
Mark's. I know it. And maybe you know it
now, being where you are with the
angels. Please forgive me Russell. I've
been unfair to you. I love Mark too, but I
chose you. We had a lot of adjustments
to make, but this next year would have
been a lot better. I was going to make it
better. Now I don't have that chance. I'm
so sorry. I'll always love you, Russell, and
cherish everything we did together.
Goodbye, my darling. Goodbye. Rest in
peace." I kissed his hands with my
blistered lips, laid my head against his
breast, and held him close for the last
time. I hated to let him go, but I knew,
looking at the empty shell of his body,
that he wasn't there. Reluctantly, I pulled
the sheet back over his face, dropped

into my wheelchair and called for Mom to come and get me.

CHAPTER THIRTY-SEVEN

I was in hospital for three days, having
my burns attended to. Mom brought
Kaitlyn to see me every day. If Russell
hadn't taken the time to wrap her in that
blanket, she would have suffered severe
burns. When he threw her through the
wall of fire, it protected her both from the
flames and from the smoke. Those extra
seconds had cost him his life, but had
saved hers. I would always be grateful to
him. Since I had lost Russell, and come so
close to losing my baby as well, I loved
her now with such a passion I could
hardly believe it. Even though I was
almost blind with my swollen eyes, it was
as if the shades had been removed from
them and I could now see clearly. I finally
saw my child for what she was – a
beautiful little girl, a treasure, a gift; all
wrapped up with gorgeous blue eyes, a
mop of curly reddish blond hair, and a
sometimes Irish temper.
    There was nothing left of the
house. I didn't even want to pick through
the charred remains looking for anything.
I had a bulldozer and loader come and
push the ruins into a pile and take them
away. I came daily to look after the
horses, but avoided looking at the black
hole where my life with Russell had been.
I stayed with Mom in her apartment. Buck

and Ying-Yang had survived the fire, and were at the Livingston farm with Marcie and Ben. Russell's brother Danny and wife Pat had come to help Ben get the hay crop in and make the funeral arrangements. Ben was in bad shape. His hair had turned white overnight. His hopes for the future of the farm were gone with the loss of Russell. Marcie was coping somewhat better, but the spark had gone out her. She was quiet and sad.

I lost everything in the fire, so I didn't have Mark's phone number at Thornhylde. I telephoned Liz at Fulmer to give her my sad news. I asked her to pass on the information to Mark. I also called my dad and told him all that had transpired. I talked to Percy and Jenny too, and they all were so shocked and saddened at my news. They asked if they should come for the funeral, but I said not to; it was such an expense. I was glad they had come for our wedding and had a chance to meet Russell on a much happier occasion.

Mark phoned me back the next night at Moms. I wept when I heard his voice. I wanted so much to just fall into his arms and be comforted. "Ah Lindsey," he said. " I am so sorry for you. I know you loved Russell truly. Only two years married. It's a hard loss for you." He paused, while I tried to regain control of my tears. "How's the wee one?"

"She's fine," I blubbered. "Russell saved her life." We talked some more, and I told him some of the details of how it happened, and of my injuries.

"Can I do anything to help you out?" Mark said. "Shall I come for the funeral? I would love to be with you to help you through this, if I could."

In answer to his first question I said, "No, not right now, thanks. I'm staying with Mom. There are a lot of details to work out, but we'll muddle through." And to his second question I replied, "No, I don't think you should, but thanks for offering.

"Well, all right" he said. "But remember, I'll be here as a friend, or more, whenever you want..." Those words gave me a jolt. They were the ones Russell used in his letter to me when he finally broke the long silence and wrote to me in England. I had quoted those same words to Mark when we were together on the bank, when Kaitlyn was conceived, but I never thought he would remember them, word for word.

I didn't know what to say. I was quiet for a moment while his message penetrated my tired mind and body. Then I said, "Mark, I can't believe you remembered those words. They came from Russell at a time when I couldn't make up my mind whether or not to stay in England or come home. They're coming back to haunt me again. I don't know what to do."

Mark said softly. "They're not a threat sweetheart, they're a promise. Go slow, and get through one day at a time. When you feel ready, bring the little one and come for a visit. I'd love to see you."

I thanked him, and we said our goodbyes.

Somehow we all got through the funeral and burial, and the get together of family and friends at Russell's house. Almost all of the same people that had come to our wedding were there to say farewell to Russell and lend me their support. I wished Dad and his family could have come, and Mark too, but it wasn't practical.

The neighbors were wonderful. They organized a benefit dance and silent auction that raised a nice sum of money for Kaitlyn and me. Russell had life insurance, and our mortgage was insured, so it was paid off on his death. I was all right financially.

When Mom went back to work, I stayed with Marcie and Ben for a while. I preferred being on the farm, and it was good for them to have their granddaughter around. She was such a bright little ray of sunshine; we couldn't be sad for long when we were around her. My hands were healing, and with heavy gloves on, I could drive the tractor and feed the cows, and help with the milking. Danny and Pat had to return to their jobs after the funeral so I was happy to do some of the chores that Russell would have done for his dad.

Still, there was a great emptiness where Russell had been. Nothing was the same without him; the table at mealtimes, the golden buckskin horse without a rider, the old truck that he loved and faithfully kept running, and especially, for me, my bed at night. Kaitlyn often woke up crying in the night, calling for her daddy. I knew she missed Russell too. I think she had nightmares about the fire, although she couldn't tell me what was wrong. I would take her into bed with me and cuddle her until her fears subsided. It helped both of us to have someone to hold and love.

I bought a new modular home and had it moved onto the acreage before winter set in. I was sad that Russell wasn't here to share it with me, as it had been his idea to get rid of the old house and move into something more modern. The Fire Marshall and insurance adjustors had said that the cause of the fire was faulty wiring. It was probably the washer and dryer running in the basement that overheated the wiring.

I asked Mom if she would like to come and live with me, and she agreed. Everyone told me not to make any big changes in my life for at least a year, and I thought it was probably good advice. Mark kept in touch by phone, and encouraged me to come for a visit. I wanted to see him, but decided against it. I had a lot of things to sort out in my mind, and I needed time to heal.

I put an ad in the paper for riding pupils, and got three girls who came every Saturday for instruction on Redwing, Figgy and Sunny. Over the winter, I started training Desert Rose and found her as apt a pupil as her brother Desert Fire had been. She was easy to train; a fluid, beautiful mover with a marvelous mind. She was a joy to work with. I did some training with Willy, the colt too. He was easier to handle now as a yearling gelding, and I worked with him on his leading manners, trailer loading, walking over obstacles and ponying him on trail rides. I was going to start him under saddle and sell him in the spring as a two year old.

When my birthday rolled around on April 15th, I gave some thought to being a widow and a single mother at age twenty-three. I had started to re-build a life, centered on horse training. I wondered if I should get back into show jumping with my mares. Then all that changed again

with some sad news and some happy
news.

Kaitlyn and I had been over at
Marcie and Ben's place for lunch. When I
had let my restless little one down to go
and play, Marcie told me quietly,
"Lindsey, we've decided to sell the place.
We have an agent coming this afternoon
to list it for us." I was shocked.

"What? You're not going to move
away, are you? You've been a part of this
community for so long. And we...Katie
and I...we need you here!" I blurted.

Marcie smiled sadly. "Well, Ben and
I have talked it over many times. As much
as we hate to move away, we can't keep
running the farm any longer. We were
going to build a little retirement cottage
on the place when you and Russell took
over this big house, but...of
course...that's all changed now." Her eyes
filled with tears and Ben took her hand
lovingly. He said, "I haven't got the heart
for it anymore, Lindsey. I miss Russell too
much, as I know you do too. I appreciate
all the help you've given me with the
chores, but it's too big a job for me now.
I want to get out of it. I'm tired."

I took both of their hands. They
were so dear to me, and I didn't want
them to leave, but I could fully
understand why they needed to go.

"You have to do what you feel is
right," I told them. "And, if the time is

right, then you should sell, although I'll miss you terribly."

Well, that was the sad news. That night at supper Mom surprised me with something brighter. Even though it was happy news, I ended up crying. We were having our tea and sharing the last of my birthday cake, when Mom said, "Lindsey, Paul has asked me to marry him."

I looked up at her in surprise. "Oh Mom! That's wonderful! He's such a nice man." Then I said, "You said 'yes;' didn't you?"

She smiled that motherly smile at me. "Well, I wanted to talk to you first. I want to know if you'll be okay if I move away. He wants me to come to live in Seattle." All of a sudden I was devastated. I wanted so much for Mom to be happy, but I didn't want to be left alone here. My pain was still too near the surface. I started to weep. Mom came around the table and put her arms around me. "I won't go as long as you still need me."

"It's not that, Mom," I blurted. I want you to go, and I want you to be happy. I like Paul and I think he's good for you," I wiped my teary eyes and sniffed. "Today, Marcie and Ben told me that they are listing the farm. They're going to move closer to Danny and Pat, in Surrey."

"Oh, my poor darling," Mom said. "We've hit you with a double whammy today, haven't we?" I nodded, trying to stop the tears. Mom ran her fingers through my hair, which felt wonderful. I missed those intimate touches between lovers. All of a sudden, my thoughts flew to Mark and the way I felt when he touched me. Mom must have been a mind reader.

"Why don't you go to Mark?" she said softly. "What's keeping you back? You know he loves you and wants you to come. There's nothing here for you anymore."

"I'm trying to make a life here, where my family is." I said stubbornly. Everyone has told me not to make a decision for at least a year, so that's why I stayed. I wanted to run to Mark right away, but it didn't seem decent." I turned to Mom and looked at her pleadingly. "It's been almost a year. Do you think it would be okay now?"

"Absolutely!" she said. "You need to be with him, and your daughter needs her father." I looked at her in amazement. She knew!

"How long have you known?" I asked, astounded. Mom grinned and handed me a tissue.

"Well, on your wedding day, I thought that you were going to leave Russell at the altar and run away with Mark. I could see that something was going on between you two. I wondered if he was here to stop your marriage, but then you went ahead and married Russell, and seemed to be happy with him." Mom sipped her tea and looked at me thoughtfully. She continued, "When you had an unplanned baby so quickly, I wondered again if Mark had anything to do with it...so...I just kept quiet and watched... I could see the resemblance quite early." Mom was smiling now, and so was I.

"Mom, you're a genius!" I threw my arms around her and hugged her. "Let's go get married to the men we love."

CHAPTER THIRTY-EIGHT

I booked a flight to London immediately. Mark was delighted when I told him that the 'wee one' and I were coming for a visit. Mom accepted Paul's proposal. They were going to have a Justice of the Peace union in Seattle, and then go on holiday to Hawaii. He was willing to wait until Mom and I got the property sold and our affairs settled.

Kaitlyn and I arrived at Heathrow Airport early in the morning. It had been a long flight trying to keep a two-year-old quiet and amused. I was tired out and Kaitlyn was crabby, having been wakened to disembark from the plane. Mark was there to meet us, and he pulled us into his large embrace. He kissed me quickly, and rolled his eyes, grinning at the squirming, fussing baby. He took our baggage tags and went off to find our luggage while I took Katie into the washroom to change her and freshen up. She was toilet trained, but I had her in diapers for the long flight. Back out into the crowds, Mark steered us out the doors towards a taxi.

"Where's your car?" I asked him, as we were bundled into the yellow cab.

"Paddington Station," Mark told the driver, and then to me he said, "Oh, I left it at Wellington. I thought we'd take the train. It's only a wee bit longer, and I booked a compartment to ourselves so Kaitlyn can move around and play. I was thinking she'd be awful restless, coming off an eight hour flight and being stuffed into a small car for two more hours." I looked at him in dismay.

"Well, I'll be damned!" I said. "I didn't know you knew anything about kids. That was very nice of you. Thanks." I gave him a sweet smile.

He gave me that crooked grin back, the exact one that Kaitlyn gave me when she was being mischievous. "You'll remember that I'm from a big family. I've had little brothers and sisters for as long as I can remember, and I've got a passel of nieces and nephews now too. I know a thing or two about kids, I do."

Mark's Irish lilt and his odd expressions charmed me immediately, as they had done before. I loved the sound of his voice.

We couldn't talk much until we got settled into a private compartment on the train. Kaitlyn had fun climbing up and down on the seats and looking out of the window. She could say quite a few words; even putting some phrases together. She excitedly pointed out cows, horses, trucks and other things she recognized as we pulled out into the beautiful green summer countryside. Mark couldn't keep his eyes off her, and I wondered what he was thinking.

When Kaitlyn grew tired of looking out at the passing countryside, Mark reached into his bag and produced a cuddly teddy bear, and held it out to her. She took it solemnly, turning it over and over. She showed us where the bear's eyes, nose and mouth were; his legs, arms and tummy.

I said to Kaitlyn, "Can you say 'thank-you' to your daddy for the bear?"

Mark glanced at me, and said, "What did you say?"

Kaitlyn looked right at her father and said clearly, "Tank-you, daddy." Mark was silent, transferring his gaze from me to his child. He stared at her in fascination.

I said, "She's your daughter, Mark. We could have her genetically tested, but I'm positive she is." He had been holding his breath, and he let it out audibly.

"Jaysus! I've wondered about her ever since you told me you were pregnant. Why didn't you tell me?" His intense blue eyes turned misty.

I looked at him shyly. "I wasn't sure at first, and then I just never got the chance, I guess. It wouldn't have changed anything while Russell was alive. I just didn't know that 'till death do us part' would come so soon."

"Aye." Mark nodded. "It's hard to believe that Russell is gone...and it's hard to believe I'm a father! Oh yes, I can see it...she's a wee McTaggart! I'm her father!"

Mark held out his arms to Kaitlyn. "Will ye come to your daddy?" he asked softly. My darling little girl that had been Russell's sweetheart must have felt some missing link fall into place. She raised her arms to Mark and let herself be lifted up and cuddled by this total stranger. She hugged her teddy bear to her, and snuggled down into Mark's arms and fell asleep, while he gazed at her adoringly. Mark put his other arm around me and pulled me close. "Ah, my little Canada," he whispered, kissing me gently. "We're together at last." I laid my cheek against his and sighed.

"Yeah...it sure feels good to be with you." I kissed him softly along his jaw line, from ear to chin. "I've missed you more that you'll ever know," I whispered back. "And I'll show you how much when I'm not so tired. Right now, I really need a snooze." I closed my eyes, and let the rhythm of the train lull me to sleep.

I awoke when the train slowed for the Wellington Station. It felt weird to be disembarking at the spot where four years ago, I had stood with Mark, smiling and waving to the shocked faces of Joan, Britt-Marie, and Donnie. A lot of water had gone under the bridge since then. I'd had a lover, been married, had a baby, and lost my husband, all in those four short years. It was no wonder I was not fully recovered yet.

Driving into Thornhylde, I felt like I was coming home. I had loved this place right from the start. I could see that Mark had made vast improvements to the grounds and house. It was wonderful that he had kept it, and made it his home. When I asked him what happened to the idea of fixing it up and selling it he replied, "I had the feeling that you'd come back some day, and knowing how much you liked the old place, I decided to keep it. I'm so glad I did. I love it too."

In fact, Mark couldn't wait to show me all the changes he had made. We dumped my luggage at the bottom of the stairs, and went immediately outside to see the new barn and paddocks he had made for the horses. With help from some fellows in the village, Mark had built a modest stable with four box stalls, four tie stalls, and a feed and tack room. He had put in a small training pen and an outdoor arena big enough for jumping practice. The estate was eighty acres in size. Mark had fenced in ten acres of orchard, meadows and forest as pasture and roaming area for the horses. Clearly, he intended to make this his home.

With Kaitlyn between us holding onto our hands, we slowly strolled out to the pasture to see Merlin and Desert Fire. As we walked, I felt such a strong bond with Mark and the beauty of our surroundings. I knew that I wanted to share this life with him.

When Kaitlyn spotted Desert Fire coming towards us, she dropped our hands and ran to the fence, crying, "Rosie, Rosie!" She climbed up on the railing and reached out her arms to the gray gelding. "Up!" she demanded to Mark.

Mark laughed with delight, and swept her up in his arms onto the back of the gentle horse. I stood by Desert Fire's head, stroking his nose and getting reacquainted. "Kaitlyn," I said, "This is Desert Fire, not Desert Rose."

"Rosie!" she insisted, shaking her head. Mark and I just laughed, wondering how to explain to a two year old that Rosie, back in Canada, had an almost identical brother in England.

With the horses following us, we walked leisurely down to the river and around the gardens. I moved along as if in a dream with Mark's arm around me. Everything looked beautiful. It was as if God had buttered the land with sunshine. Even the thorny hedges were beautiful, protective; strong. In a flash of memory that was instantly illusive, I knew this place as if in another lifetime, and it was home.

That night, after a delicious roast beef dinner, Mark and I sat close together by the fireside. Kaitlyn wouldn't stay in the nursery by herself in the cot that Mark had bought for her. She had screamed bloody blue murder every time I tried to tiptoe out. I explained to Mark how she was still having nightmares about the fire, and that she usually slept with me. He didn't mind, so we brought her back downstairs where she had fallen asleep on the sofa, with her new teddy tucked under her arm.

"Shall we move the cot into our room?" he asked. "Or, am I assuming too much by thinking that you would like to sleep with me? There are other bedrooms, if you prefer." For once, he wasn't teasing; he was being serious.

"Let's go move the cot," I said with a grin. "I didn't come all this way to sleep alone. I've missed you so much, Mark." The longing was evident in my voice. We slid into each other arms then and kissed ardently. The old passion was still there, simmering like a delectable pot of stew on the back burner. I held Mark's face in my hands and looked into his deep blue eyes. "I want to be with you," I said, "but I still have a lot of guilt...about you...about Russell...about the fire."

Mark said, "Let it go, Lindsey, let it go love. It's all in the past now". He kissed me again. I wasn't quite ready to let it drop.

"Mark?

"Hmmm?"

"I need to tell you this."

"Okay..." He stopped kissing me and looked into my eyes expectantly.

"I was to blame for Russell losing his life. I left the dryer running in the basement. Russell was always worried about the wiring in that old house. And then...I was away when the fire broke out. I went for a ride down the dyke on Redwing. Katie was sleeping, and I left her alone in the house. I had never done that before."

Mark sat up. He was paying attention now. These were details he hadn't known about. Tears welled up in my eyes and trickled down my cheeks. "He was over at the farm cutting hay. I think we both saw the smoke at the same time, and we both raced for the house. Redwing jumped the bank and the back fence like a steeplechaser! Russell got there just a little ahead of me. If I hadn't doused myself in the horse trough I would have been burned a lot worse." Mark kissed the burn scars on my hands." Go on, " he said. "Tell me all about it."

"Russell wrapped Kaitlyn in a blanket and threw her to me. I ran out with her, and then he got caught in the fire as the walls started to fall in. It's all my fault that he died." Sobs shook my body as I slumped against Mark. He held me, and rocked me gently. My voice was muffled against his chest. "He was crazy about Kaitlyn. I don't know if he ever suspected that she wasn't his own. I was so unfair to him. I really screwed up my marriage!"

Like that night back in the cottage, when I was so upset about Russell, Mark held me until I cried myself out. Then he disentangled himself from me, and rose to put some more wood on the fire. He turned to face me as I wiped my tears on my sleeve and forced myself to stop sniveling.

"Now listen to me, Lindsey, and I'll tell you what I think about this," he said. I listened. We had never talked about spiritual matters before, but I was to realize that Mark had a unique blend of belief, consisting of Christianity, eastern philosophy and Irish mysticism. "Do you believe in destiny?" he asked me.

"I don't know what to believe in anymore. I'm all mixed up."

"Well then, I think that Russell was meant to die by some means. If it hadn't been the fire, it would have been an accident of some kind. You are meant to be with me. That's why we have a child. There are many things going on in our lives and around us that we are not even aware of; things in other dimensions."

This opened my mind to new possibilities. I said, "You mean like spiritual guides or angels changing the course of our lives?"

Mark nodded. "Aye."

"But why did he have to die? Why couldn't I just leave him or something?"

"I don't know the answer to that except that his time on this earth plane was done. You have to accept that, and realize that nothing was your fault. It was all pre-planned by some greater order of life, without your knowledge. It was all meant to be. You have to forgive yourself, and move on. Do you understand what I'm saying?"

"You're saying that God wanted him for some other mission?"

"Sure, something like that. He was called away, so you could be with me. Let go of him, and let go of who was to blame. It doesn't matter anymore." Mark came and knelt beside me. He took both of my hands in his. "I love you Lindsey, and Kaitlyn too. I want to marry you. Will you stay, and be the Mistress of Thornhylde?"

A little smile tickled the corners of my mouth. "I love you too Mark. I'll not be your 'Mistress', but I would love to be your wife." A great surge of joy flowed through me as I melted into Mark's arms again. I felt my burdens and troubles fly away. It all made sense now. I whispered against his ear, "You said you were here for me as a friend... or more, if I wanted...well, I'm ready for the 'more' part. Let's get our daughter and go on upstairs."

THE END

EPILOGUE

When I returned to Abbotsford, three weeks later, I was wearing a dazzling emerald and diamond ring. Mark wanted to give me an emerald; symbolic of the Emerald Isle and his Irish heritage. Our wedding was in the planning stages for September.

I sold Willy as a jumping prospect, and made arrangements for the remaining four horses to be boarded at Eagle Ridge under Pam's care until they could be shipped to England. I had protested to Mark about the fortune it was going to cost to bring them all over, but he reminded me that he *had* a fortune, so it didn't matter.

We sold the acreage quickly, and Mom moved to Seattle to marry Paul. They were going on a cruise for their honeymoon. The Livingston's dairy farm down the road also sold in a few months. Russell's parents moved to Surrey to be close to their remaining son, Danny.

Kaitlyn and I returned to Thornhylde at the end of August with our faithful pets Ying-Yang and Buckwheat. Mark and I were married at the family estate, Leamaneh, on September 10th, 1990,with all his family present as well as Dad, Percy and Jenny, Liz and Joe from Fulmer,

and Joan Hall, who had stayed in Scotland and married a highlander. Mom and Paul were on their own honeymoon so were not at our wedding, but they were going to join us for Christmas at Thornhylde. We had telegrams and letters of congratulations from my sisters who couldn't be there, and from Britt-Marie in Kentucky and Donnie in New Zealand.
.

Two years later, an ultrasound revealed that we were expecting a baby boy. Mark asked me if I would like to call him Russell. I threw my arms around him, and said 'yes'. I wanted to keep Russell's memory alive in our family, since he had sacrificed his life for Kaitlyn.

When little redheaded Russell (or Rusty as we nicknamed him) was five, Bonnie-Jean was born; Bonnie because she was so pretty, and Jean for my mom.

Our children are now seventeen, thirteen, and eight. They are all expert riders, and are involved in Pony Club, archery, gymnastics and swimming. Mark is a loving, but stern father and these kids are not spoiled although they have a wonderful home and every advantage.

Mark has been so good to me, and he's been true to me, something I find rather wonderful, as he was quite a playboy in his younger days. We are the best of friends, and lovers still. We ride together, and go for long walks where we discuss the children and affairs of the estate.

We've been back to visit family in Canada every year, and have also enjoyed trips to France, Spain and Italy. Of course we go to Leamaneh several times a year.

My brother Percy enjoyed coming to Thornhylde for his summer holidays all through his teen years. He loved the horses, and became a good rider. Our kids in turn liked to holiday at the quaint little village of Seahouses in Northumberland. Percy and I are very close. He is married himself now, with a little daughter of his own.

Of the horses, Merlin is gone and is buried at Thornhylde, under the oaks. Kaitlyn's beloved Sundance, and my Figgy, our last links with Russell, are gone now too. Redwing is old and sway-backed at twenty-six. She and Figgy have had many foals that have all been a delight. Desert Fire is twenty, and his little sister Desert Rose is nineteen. These two are pure white with age now. All of these horses gave us so much joy, uniting Mark and I and our children with a common bond of interest and love.

My life has come full circle. I am content, with the best of both worlds. Choosing between two men and two countries was

not such an issue after all. I have them
both, in full measure. I am blessed.

ISBN 1412076536